A2 [illegible]
The Murphy Mysteries

By

Tim Shannon

Table of Contents

Dedication

This book is dedicated to my bride Peg Shannon and the boys Nathaniel Shannon, Matthew Shannon, Owen K. McNulty, and David E. Denys.

Acknowledgement

Not much happens without the help of others, and I first thank God for the life I have. I want to thank Connie Lofgren and Ben Hunt for the inspiration they provided to get this project done. I'm grateful to Lorie Beardsley-Heyn and Pete Heyn for providing editing and encouragement. I especially wish to thank Nathaniel Shannon and Sean Madigan Hoen for their help throughout this venture.

Foreword

One would assume that universities and colleges are safe with little or no crime other than thefts of bicycles, laptops, or backpacks. This is far from the truth, as there are many heinous crimes even in upscale, economically well-off communities-crimes not perpetrated by outsiders and predators roaming the campus but by well-educated individuals who are narcissistic and lack compassion and empathy for others.

It is just as likely that crimes are investigated and solved by trained professionals who work together. This book highlights inter-agency cooperation, education, networking, and the camaraderie of those in Public Safety Agencies who sacrifice much to keep their communities safe so others may live with minimal fear.

The Death Knell was equivalent to a public announcement transmitted by the community Bell Tower back in the Middle Ages. It usually marked someone's passing.

Chapter 1

The house phone rang. Rolling over, looking at the clock, and picking up the handset, I could barely hear Lt. Srennock say, "There's a dead guy in the men's room, basement level of Hill Auditorium. You need to come in." Pat didn't stir, part of the coma-like state after hours of the Hallmark channel and Sudoku.

I dressed and ambled down the stairs, put on a Tyvek and scuffed Rockies with booties over them. I grabbed my satchel containing my Sig 40 Smith &Wesson, 3 extra magazines, cuffs, a flashlight, a tape measure, a ball of twine, powdered dental stone and picks, fingerprint powder, lifters, batteries, a polaroid camera, and my trusty Nikon 8008. The floodlight illuminated the driveway as I walked around my 10-year-old Toyota (as was my daily practice), noticing my left front tire was low.

This was a great ride, a great bargain. I came upon it when an elderly gentleman was replacing the exhaust system. It had belonged to his invalid wife and was going for $1,100. It had 80,000 miles on it with both a radio and automatic seatbelts, so I jumped to get it. I recalled buying a new car once on time-a '79" Delta 88, 4 door-and since I'd let frugality rule when spending on clothes, sports gear and cars.

Make a note to have my tires checked and rotated at Glen's.

The car clock read 04:20 hours, but it was 05:20 hours, as one needed an engineering degree to reset it each fall and spring. State legislatures are retarded, thinking they had to write laws relating to time changes.

I hopped in, turned the key, and the engine came alive.

Less than five minutes later, I found myself instinctively pulling into Dom's drive-through, where the heir apparent to the bakery gold-mine, young Mr. Chou, handed me a fritter and medium coffee with double cream in return for two bucks.

The coffee burned my lips but woke me up. I'd never acquired the taste for dark roast French roast or the current politically correct beverages-lavender scented lattes and so on-and as a result, I saved a bunch of money.

Westbound and down Washtenaw, missing all 18 lights and two stop signs, I rolled to a stop on Ingalls at the circle drive to Hill Auditorium. Three uniformed officers were milling around the building. Some pranksters had dumped dish soap in Cooley Fountain, and suds were flowing over the sides.

"Make a note to set up a sniper in the Bell Tower on that fountain, and that would put an end to that BS."

Lieutenant Srennock nodded as I came in and motioned to take the stairs as she joined me.

El-Tee, aka Natasha Srennock, was tall and lean. She came into the department the same year as me, was married and had one son. Her husband, an undertaker, thought he was a player and stepped out on her, and she finally divorced him. Then she identified a switch in her orientation, finding the company of other women more appealing. The hoot was: the DB lieutenant, a retired State Police Team Leader, had no use for female cops and often would say, "Murph, they all need to go back to the kitchen." "So much for diversity at the U." Officer Stretch, a very jolly individual nearly 7 feet tall was our diverse token giant, ducked at the men's room door as we entered.

"How goes it Stretch?" I said.

Ofc. Stretch replied, " Good, The corpse is in the stall, took one in the melon. The guy didn't have the decency to close his eyes, so his sunken orbs were staring at everything we did."

When I first started out in a small rural hamlet, the senior policeman Fletcher Donaldson of the SLPD told me murders are the easiest to solve, "At the autopsy, you just remove the cornea," he said, steering his cruiser down a county road, me in the passenger seat, farmland reeling by at a high rate of speed. "The murderer's image will be imprinted on the cornea, and it's the last thing they saw before they died."

"Is that so," I replied. "You solved a lot of murders in this sleepy town of 5,000? What if the guy jumped you from behind? Does that theory still hold true, or does he have to have eyes in the back of his head, also?"

Fletch babbled something about the rookie thinking he knows it all and crossed the centerline, letting me know he—the old veteran—was still in charge, and he could scare the hell out of me, but I often did that myself while driving; Fortunately, I liked to keep anyone riding shotgun on high alert when I was driving.

Ten years later and I'm standing in this University rest room looking down at a fresh corpse: Mid-forties, white male, 5'10" and around 200 pounds, with a full beard and closely, cut black hair. He had a hematite band on his right ring finger and dirt under his fingernails. At the bridge of his nose was a single hole, likely a gunshot at close range. There was some stippling on the skin. Almost no blood was present, and what was there was sticky and gelatinized to the point where lividity was setting in. I guessed I could rule out "death by natural causes," which left homicide, suicide or an accident.

Lieutenant briefed me on what they'd gathered: "John Buzzard, the building manager, found him at 12:30 am and not having a working cell phone on him, didn't call until 12:50 am. Buzzard thought it was a staged prank before realizing it was a real stiff."

Lieutenant Srennock then related, "No one except

Buzzard was here when we arrived, so we secured the perimeter, then called the deputy chief who said to call you. We also called for an investigator from the Medical Examiner's office."

"No one touched anything, and Buzzard, nor any of us know the guy. I must run, day shift briefing in 20 minutes. I'll leave the units here until after briefing."

"Thanks, "I said, "You'll know when I know."

We nodded at each other, and she ambled off into the darkness as I heard her footsteps drifting off on the marble stairs.

Often, I dealt with Lt. Srennock and my mind drifted momentarily to another incident. One fall afternoon, when the epicenter of the ethnocentric brain trust of the Republic had shifted to the football stadium, I was working my normal plain clothes detail, targeting ticket scalpers, weed users and public leakers and lurkers. I was dispatched to once again meet with Srennock's road cops. One veteran officer found a guy hanging in a stairwell of a campus building. She said to me, "I got to go notify the family and was wondering if you'd go with me as you're... sensitive with this stuff?"

"Yeah, right," I thought.

I'd learned a lot about sensitivity from the best, a city cop named Verdi who said his mother didn't like the name

Green, so gave him the Latin version of it, even though he had red hair and a pasty complexion. Verdi had a square jaw, piercing blue eyes, and large hands and often articulated the humor in humanity. He and I rode together back in the pre-politically correct days. We once rolled on a dead guy who'd had the audacity to pull his canary yellow VW bug into his neighbor's attached garage, close the door and asphyxiate himself.

That occurred in the dead of January, during a midwinter thaw. The owners called when they smelled rotting flesh and checked their garage to find the late, great Jacque Daly frozen to the steering wheel. A missing person report was made four days prior when he and his vintage '72 yellow VW bug failed to show up at home.

So, Command was called, Captain BT Bubbles rolled out of his cruiser and stood erect, displaying a massive rotund frame, jowls that nearly covered his collar brass. After a big group hug with the neighbors, he asked the distressed homeowner, "Would you have any coffee?" Within minutes a dozen neighbors were strangely present in a circle as Captain Bubbles ranked this incident against others he'd witnessed, saying, "This isn't much." After all, we were up by Barton Dam, where in a storage shed, we'd found the remains of some guy's wife filleted in a dozen cases of quart-size Mason Jars. It was as if he was canning for the winter.

Standing in an alcove away from Captain Bubbles'

audience, I laughed so hard I damn near pissed my pants and was unable to control myself as we walked across the street to a large two-story colonial to notify the family in this upscale neighborhood.

Expressing irreverence, I asked Verdi, "So what do you say, we found him, and he's now a Popsicle?"

"No, be sensitive," Verdi replied. "Remember, this is the Republic; ask her if she's 'the Widow Daly' and let her know he'll make a great third base now!"

Holding in an avalanche of laughter was like trying to stop yourself from vomiting; you know you'll feel better after you get it out. So I'd learned from the finest; even if there didn't seem to be an ounce of sensitivity in my heart, I sure knew how to pretend. Of course, my heart had softened over time. That is what a professional does: speak from the heart even if you don't have one. And I wasn't sure I did back then.

The door opened, and Ms. Daly's look told us she already knew, but she invited us in, our hats-in hand expressing the requisite sentiment for the occasion, "sorry for your loss." I thought, *Wow, what a beautiful house* with Wedgewood china, Bleek figurines on the fireplace mantel, 19th Century oak, maple and cherry furniture and a masterful copy of an Edward Church painting, and a dozen portraits of young men set on the built-in bookshelves, The widow looked worn, early-sixties with too much makeup, but I'd learned from my wife along the way—they don't do it to look pretty but to feel pretty. I did know that at some point, I'd be meeting this guy's family and needed to learn empathy and sympathy.

We delivered the news. She grabbed a figurine of Little Boy Blue off the mantel and threw it with the velocity of a major league pitcher, screaming, "That son of a bitch."

It hit the wall and shattered.

While finishing up with the widow, an ebony-skinned-teenage male came down the grand staircase and said, "Oh good, I get the car." He ran out the door and across the street in search of his inheritance.

In questioning the widow, she'd admitted their marriage was on the rocks. The teen who wandered through was adopted as a two-year-old when the deceased was a missionary in the Congo. (Or maybe he was a bio-child?)

The bank account was empty, you know?" said the Widow Daly, tears welling up in her eyes. She mumbled, "Bastard," and picked up a Wedge-wood vase.

I cautioned, "Throw it if it makes you feel better, its normal to be angry in these situations," Verdi looked at me with a dour expression conveying how uncomfortable he was trying to console her.

She nodded and threw an inside curve, nailing the fireplace grate before porcelain ricocheted all over the carpet.

Her voice trembled as she said, “We now have nothing. He had a gambling habit and traveled to the casinos in Windsor every week. I’ll have to sell the house.”

Verdi closed out the conversation by expressing our sympathies, and we headed back to the patrol car, leaving Captain Bubbles to his community-policing program.

Chapter 2

After a long delay at Hill Auditorium, Medical Examiner Investigator A. Richard Scribbins arrived and said, "Since he caught one in the melon, he likely died of lead poisoning and a large headache as there is no exit hole."

"Yeah, I got eyes and can see that," I said.

Scribbens interrupted my next thought, saying, "I'd be looking for someone with a gun, like a .22 rifle or pistol?" He used his usual sarcasm, "You're the Dick, go Dick around and find out."

Scribbens was an odd one, spent a score of years as a trooper and gave it up to run an ambulance company and show up at fatal crashes. He had a certain charm. When training others, he kept a syringe full of water in his coat to wake up folks who failed to pay attention to him. We did our thing, and it was nearly 7 a.m. when the crime scene sketch, photos, measurements and interviews were done, and the deceased was searched and hauled away.

His property inventory revealed:

One Motorola flip-phone (likely got at a fire sale)

Two best keys on a ring with a beehive stamped on a metal tag. The keys were stamped-

'U of M- Do Not Duplicate,"

One black comb

One two-month metal token from a Twelve-Step fellowship.

Stretch came down with the facility manager- James Buzzard (pronounced Boozer, with the emphasis on the second syllable), who had the appearance of a zombie. He had very sallow, ruddy skin, high cheekbones, close-set eyes and a v-shaped scar on his cheek, 150 lbs. and 6'7", could have had a career in horror films.

"So, Mr. Buzzard, quite a shock, I'm sure. Can you walk us through what brought you in here on a Saturday?" I said.

Buzzard looked away from the corpse and replied, "The Republic Symphony played here last night. I got here around noon and set everything up as their rehearsal was at 6 pm, and the performance was at 8 p.m. I was here from around 1:30 p.m. until I did my rounds after the building closed. I think that was around 10:30 p.m., and I went to my office and looked up things on the computer and went over the list of things I need to do for the beginning of the week."

Likely looking at porn, I thought, but no sense in bringing that up now.

"Were you alone?" I asked.

"Of course, I don't work with anybody else. I like having

this building to myself."

"I came down here about 1:15 to 1:30 a.m. to turn off the lights as I was done for the day. That's when I found him. They don't look real, do they? I thought it was a mannequin at first, sort of like one of those rescue Annie dolls." He winced. "It was just too weird, once I saw his face and his eyes were still open—I'm never going to forget that. My cell phone doesn't work down here, and I haven't charged it, and the battery was dead. It was hard to focus on anything else, so I went all the way back to my office and called from there."

"You know this guy?" I said.

"No, never saw him before. I'd remember his face if I had."

"I don't suppose you heard any noises or voices on this end of the building?"

"No, I was just totally shocked."

"Do you know what happened to him?" Buzzard asked

Looking at Buzzard's body language and his face, the usual plausible deniability instinct kicked in, and I said, "With that hole in his face. We figure he didn't die of natural causes. When was the last time you were down here in the men's room?"

Buzzard said, "Tuesday night, they had a get-together in

that open area for all the ushers and staff to celebrate the end of the season. I came through but didn't stay. I came back through about 9 o'clock that night to make sure everyone was gone and locked up.”

"Hey, Sarge, I need to eat something,” Stretch yelled. Stretch was diabetic, and shift work was tough on eating and sleeping habits, especially working midnights.

“Okay, call the area car over to relieve you, and then you can call it a day, thanks for not mucking up the scene, like Inspector Bluett always did, moving things and stepping in shit and then blaming anyone else as he was known to do. “ Stretch was a good road officer; he took investigations as far as he felt comfortable and then, wanting the detectives to have something to do, would turn the investigations over to us.

His paperwork was accurate, and he didn’t do a lot of griping about the department.

As we were in the basement, I started pulling trash out of the cans on this level and found nothing. This was just as I’d learned 30 years prior on a slow Saturday dayshift after being called over to a building where a security guard found a suspicious guy wandering the halls.

Outside a lab in the hall was a broken window. When questioned, the guy claimed to be a custodial supervisor, which made no sense as they all worked Monday-through-Friday. When asked for ID, he looked up, saw a sign with the acronym ERIC and said his name was Eric. When asked his last name, his response was, "Sevareid." *Of course,* I thought, *one of the top newscasters in the world moonlights as a custodial supervisor.* Eric Sevareid was an uncommon name; there was only the well-known WWII correspondent and newscaster.

When asked for ID, he said it was in his car. He walked to the door and dumped a rag containing something in a trashcan. So we went out to his car, and on the backseat, partially covered with a blanket, was an IBM Selectric II with a State Police property tag on it. So we hooked him up and dug through the trash to find rubber feet for a typewriter that someone had moved in an office, a fishing knife with a 5" blade stuck in his waistband, and a sparkplug wire routinely used to break safety glass, one of a score of times where trash pulls helped solve the caper.

Later I learned this guy had balls, as he'd walked into the State Police Headquarters on Harrison Ave in E. Lansing, advised he was there about fixing a typewriter, said he had to take it back to his shop, and walked out with it. I flinched as my cellphone rang.

"Scribbens here, autopsy with Dr. Red at the Pathology Department tomorrow at 9 AM."

I returned to the scene. Buzzard was mopping the area. "Hey, too bad he caused more work for you," I said. "I was wondering, did you happen to hear a gunshot by any chance?”

Buzzard glared at me with his beady little eyes and said as if irritated, “No, I would have told you if I had.”

I checked another trashcan and found nothing useful.

“The tunnel entrance still behind the storage room?” “Yes, I was in there when I first came in yesterday.”

“Any reason you didn’t mention that earlier?

“You didn’t ask,” Buzzard snapped.

“Why were you in there?” I kept an even tone. I had to make a note of this, as the tunnel doors were normally all alarmed.

“I was looking for another storage area for all these chairs until the guys from Property Disposition got them,” he said in an irritated tone, turning his back to me, hunched over the mop bucket.

“What about the alarm?”

“It was disarmed years ago by orders of the general foreman for the plant department, “ Standing straight up and glaring at me.

“Didn’t know that,” I said. “Any idea why?”

“Yup, there was a crew of trades guys, including their foremen, who stashed their booze there, and they didn’t want the alarms going off so security would respond."

Turning on my trusty 30-year-old Kel-Lite, I swept the beam from side to side. I covered the tunnel from Hill Auditorium to the Natural Science Building and found one left boot print measuring about Size 7 made by what looked like a Vibram sole;

2 cigarette butts; and, around the circle of chairs used for the TGIF parties, a vintage 1974 edition of *Hustler*, Magazine, which would garner $250 on eBay by now.

On the floor were four one-inch wheel marks in the dirt. Pulling out a Polaroid, I snapped a few pictures and then shot a whole roll of 400DX with the Nikon 8008. I felt satisfied with the morning thus far. After bagging and tagging the cigarette butts and magazines, I realized how hot and humid those tunnels were, over 100 degrees.

I remembered poor Chuck Beasley.

One very nice spring day on campus, when 80% of the tradesmen in the area were scoping out the female sunbathers, one guy was actually working. Chuck Beasley, a pipefitter and welder, was 100 yards into the tunnel welding a seam when he had a heart attack, fell forward on the weld seam and burned the flesh on his chest as he expired. The ambient temperature was 122 in that tunnel, and the accident triggered a MIOSHA investigation lasting the better part of a year.

Under my Kevlar vest, sweat was pouring down my spine now, just like that summer day ten years prior.

I secured my Kel-Lite, which was a relic, but it caused a lot of controversy in its day. Back in the late '60s, LA County Deputy Sheriff Dan Kellor developed this tool to replace the nightstick, and it sold well. It was the preferred tool, or shall I say weapon. Mine was only a 3-D Cell black anodized aluminum case, whereas another associate, Pieter Schmenke, carried a 6-D cell flashlight to increase his distance from any problem.

The controversy occurred when one of the infamous California Highway Patrolman needed to get voluntary compliance from a trucker he pulled over; but not wanting to cap the road jockey, he dorked him on the noggin with his Kel-Lite and fractured the poor soul's skull. Lawsuits came fast and furious after that, and departments moved away from issuing them and even prohibited carrying them. We didn't have a policy about carrying them, so I wasn't in violation.

One muggy July night after a storm, branches fell off the trees from the high winds, and I was patrolling the Diag when I found one of the local street urchins wandering around with a six-foot branch. A young guy, a kid really, his name was Andy, and he was drunk and threatening people strolling the original, park-like forty acres of campus, known as the Diag after the bars closed.

When I approached him, he yelled, “Damn Pig,” and swung the branch, barely missing me. I told him, “Time to leave.”

“Screw you!” he said and swung the limb again, nearly grazing me. His follow-through was that of Tiger Woods on rum, and he left the entire “6 position” open (from when I once fenced exposed), so I used my trusty Kel-lite to push him back. But he lunged forward, and I struck him squarely on the forehead. It sounded like a hammer striking a watermelon. He went down to the ground in a heap. When he stood up, he bolted off into the darkness.

An hour later, dispatch sent a car to the Hospital Emergency Room on a drunk who checked in complaining he’d been robbed while wandering around campus. There was a clue. My Kel-lite saved me injury on more than one occasion. As for Andy, the next summer, on July 4, he was playing music too loud in his apartment; the neighbor told him to turn it down, and when he didn’t, the neighbor blew his head off with a shotgun. Dead at twenty.

Chapter 3

After examining the tunnels, it was time to go back and talk with the bosses. It being Friday, everyone was in the break room having coffee and bagels. The chief, deputy chief, and DB Lieutenant – newly promoted to Captain, were all accounted for, so we slipped into the conference room and briefed them on what had transpired.

The chief and I sparred on rare occasions. When angry, color rose in his face, and a vein throbbed on his temple. He said, "Sgt. Murphy, you going to trim your mustache?" This was not a question but an order; somehow, he and his support staff couldn't interpret my mood if I wasn't clean-shaven. My reply was always, "Sure, boss, I'll get right on that," but I never did.

The boot print and wheel marks bothered me. I had the photos enlarged to 3x2 feet by Nathaniel's Photography so I could study both their class and accidental characteristics of them.

I also delivered all the evidence, what little there was, to the Second District State Police Lab in Northville, Michigan. It always gave me a reason to learn more from a group of folks who looked at things just a shade differently than me. They sent more letters rejecting evidence that didn't match than evidence that did-but when it matched, it was a beautiful thing.

I appreciated these unsung heroes even though they didn't make many cases I had.

I'd worked a series of burglaries where tens of thousands of dollars in computer equipment was stolen from the Business School. It was during the Christmas Holiday weekend, so few, if any, people would have been in the building, and the custodial staff hadn't been there since the Friday prior to Christmas. It was already the 29th. Susan Muzzie, the facility manager, met me at the loading dock after her report to dispatch. I checked the doors, windows, and trashcans, and the solitary item I found was a cardboard sleeve for a duffel bag in a trash bag in the hall outside the computer lab.

I rang up the Lab Print Expert Elroy Zachery, who said, "You know, Sgt. Murphy, we probably won't be able to do much with this until the Tigers are in mid-season, as there is a backlog of stuff to be processed. You know, there are 165 departments submitting evidence to us all the time."

"Ok," I replied, "no Maker's Mark for you next Christmas. I have what looks like a pristine latent thumbprint. I super glued the cardboard under the fume hood and raised the print, and photographed it. I just need you to run it through AFIS. Could you do that?"

"Bring it on up; just don't make a habit of it," he said.

Two weeks later, the official lab notice: "The prints return to a thrice convicted Romulan parolee named Leroy

Brown Russell."

Six o'clock the next morning, the State Police Fugitive Team and I keyed the door at the No Tell Motel and found him in mid-stroke with a Michigan Avenue Momma.

Nothing like a dozen weapons trained on you when you're trying to expel the bad seed. The poor guy stood sweating and panting naked as a jaybird and had nothing to show for it, all due to the prints. He was arrested, confessed, arraigned and released on bond. A week later, he overdosed on heroin in his backyard and died.

A good evidentiary case, though.

The Yacht Club, one of my favorite watering holes, was close by and had great food and friendly staff, and I could relate to the owner, who was just surly enough to appreciate my sense of humor. It was also the oasis for a number of law enforcement in the area.

I was joined then by my partner-in-mayhem, Seamus McAlroy, as he was a true Irish Catholic and a very strong family man with an incredible work ethic. I knew whatever he worked on was done well. He not only caught the bad guy but made sure the criminal case going through the system was rock solid. He was well-read and could quote literary works and their authors. He also excelled in his knowledge of the law and procedure and was noticed by management and department heads for his professional demeanor. McAlroy was good with firearms and was designated one of the first-range officers slated for the FBI National Academy and local computer crimes schools.

Seamus was 6'2", well built with red hair and a full bushy mustache. He wore cowboy boots and a shoulder holster for his Sig 226, even though his weapon of choice was a Beretta 9mm. He styled himself after a movie detective icon. He had a playful side, which sometimes bordered on psychotic as he'd wire my desk with pull-apart fireworks so that when I'd pull my lap drawer open, I'd experience a minor explosion. McAlroy just sat and laughed as I cursed him and plotted numerous ways to return the favor.

We spent nightshifts drinking on the roof of a carport and draining the vein or sitting on the Diag emptying a six-pack, trying to decompress from the stress of dealing with the politically correct snowflake crowd. Often the stress would come as the students complained and believed somehow they were special and not at risk from the local thugs who befriended them to steal, rape and rob them.

Too many reports came through where they left dorm rooms and cars full of property unlocked, laptops and purses sitting out in the open unattended, and they got drunk or high and walked through dark places with the expectation they were safe when they were extremely vulnerable. Both of us had to be as politically sensitive as we needed to be. As they were the " best and the brightest," we had to be guardians of them for the duration of their stay in the Republic. We discussed every case and enjoyed the humor of those little peevish foibles of others in the department.

He fell for a local female cop who came into the marriage with a bright little gal. We'd sit and bitch about the department, pollute our bodies with the hyper-caloric intake of deep-fried "what-ever," and make judgments with facts not in evidence because it helped us.

One weary evening at home, as the TV droned inside my living room, there was a rapping at the side door. I opened it to find Seamus standing in the rain. His face was red from dried tears, and his voice cracked, "Can I come in?"

"Absolutely, what's up?" I said.

"She served me with divorce papers. "We've ben married less than ten years, four kids, and she wants out. This was hardly a shocker, as the Barna Group had just issued statistics that for every ten couples married, six break up. She had integrity issues from the get-go, having known her prior to their marriage and saw her falsify a search of a suspect prior to an arrest as well as in the police report. This was only confirmed when she went to the dark side as an attorney defending juvenile delinquents in Detroit.

The second day into the Hill investigation, I found an extra ten minutes before the autopsy to call McAlroy.

"How goes it?" I asked.

"I'll be okay."

I didn't think so, so I kept an eye on him for what seemed like a few months hoping he wouldn't go off the deep end. Fortunately, God smiled on him, and he later found the love of his life.

Chapter 4

The next morning at zero dark thirty, I began the day with protein powder, yogurt, berries, nuts and ice-cubes mixed in the blender to aid my heart-healthy diet. The smoothie was an acquired taste, like drinking Glenfidddich straight from the bottle. Maybe a splash of that would help my disposition.

I grabbed my bag and drove on over to the local gas station, inflated the offending tire and was stopped by all sixteen lights between home and the hospital. The morgue was off the main loading dock, and I pulled in past the guard shack.

I received a warm greeting from Leonard Lawrence, who had the appearance of a member of a 6th-grade crossing guard with the AAA Safety Patrol. He was rotund, with chubby pink cheeks and short stubby hands. Exuding command presence over the loading dock, he wore a Sam Browne belt with a shoulder strap over a rumpled uniform decorated by numerous pins, the largest one declaring 43 years of dedicated service. He was a fixture at this hospital, and his claim to fame was drawing very detailed cars and planes and boats in his spare time.

"Sergeant Murphy," he said. "What brings you to this hallowed ground?"

I smiled back uncharacteristically, as previously

instructed by the Chief.

"Lenny, I just got one question for you today?"

"What's that, Sergeant?"

"Did you start this job while you were still in high school?

"No, sir, grade school."

"I'm going to the morgue. "If you see anyone escaping, call me?"

"Good one, Sergeant. I'll keep my eyes open."

I parked my wheels in a posted "No Parking" zone and went to the steel door, and pushed the call button. I expected Igor or some hunchback to let me in, but the attendant, a non-descript white guy in scrubs, buzzed me in and went back to reading his newspaper and slurping his steaming coffee.

"Is the M.E. here?"

"He's sharpening his knives," said the attendant. "He's in the other room."

I looked through the door and saw a balding red head and wiry 6'6" frame. He was slicing paper with what appeared to be an 18" long serrated bread knife. The M.E. looked up and waved for me to enter.

I walked in and smiled again, as instructed, I extended my hand. The M.E. greeted me and then launched into the merits of the knife in his hand. He explained they were carving knives made of Swedish steel and called a "Cattleman's knife" and sold for $75.00 each.

I followed him back to the cutting room and found the lab attendant had the Corpus Delecti laid out on a grossing station. This was a stainless table with holes so the fluids could run off. There was an antiseptic smell to the room, but I knew a perforation of the GI tract might result in an infusion of unpleasant odors. My remedy was oil of peppermint liberally applied to my mustache to deaden the smells of decomposition.

The M.E. said, "Tell me about what you found?"

"We found the body in the men's room stall with what appeared to be a hole just at the bridge of his nose right between the eyes. It appeared he had been shot at close range as there was powder stippling on his skin. No gun or much other evidence there."

The M.E. started a running commentary for the recording device, describing the condition of the corpse and its unique characteristics. He described the general physical characteristics as well as the condition of his skin, scars, marks and tattoos, one being a two-inch bird of prey with large talons on his left buttocks in black and green and red and a hooded figure on his right upper arm.

The M.E. and I discussed the 1/8th inch hole between his eyes and the rather sunken condition of the eye socket. Holding the right eyelid open, the good doctor grabbed a syringe with a four-inch needle on it and immediately stuck it through the man's right eye lens, extracting fluid from the vitreous humor, the jelly-like substance in the eye. At my first autopsy, I nearly heaved watching this, but I was used to it now.

Some air in the syringe made a slight sucking noise, only adding to the stomach-churning ambiance of the room. This sample would be used for a two-fold analysis of the potassium in his body. This helps to fix the time of death and chemical changes in electrolytes in the cells after death.

I remembered another time when I brought one of the rookie Dickless Tracies along, and she turned ashen and green, having to step out of the room during this procedure. Once the eyeball was removed and cut open, the M.E. and I both agreed it very much resembled an oyster on the half shell. Today, all this was making me hungry.

The doctor then took his scalpel and made an incision behind the head, and pushed the scalp and skin up over his face with some difficulty so he could get to his skull. The skull saw whirled as he made a circle around his cranium with what looked like a Dremel Moto-tool but was a very fine bone saw showering little chips and dust onto his arm. The grinding from the saw noise made me think of 7th Grade woodshop with ten other pre-pubescent boys learning to use various tools.

I was jolted back to the present when he popped the skullcap off like opening the lid on the Friar Tuck cookie jar in my boyhood kitchen. He exposed the Dura mater and then, underneath, folds of the actual brain.

Probing around the brain, he found dark coagulated blood and what appeared to be a hemorrhage located deep in the center of the brain. What looked like a small pebble was lodged in the third ventricle. Using a pair of plastic tweezers, he prodded and pulled until it came free, and he dropped it in the dish with a plop, the good doctor saying with some satisfaction, “There you go, Sergeant!”

So this was it, a 40-grain Magnum hollow point with barely any deformity. It ended the four-plus decades of this man’s hopes, dreams, and accomplishments.

“Like blades of grass, we wither and die.”

I bagged and tagged it and put it in my vest pocket. A professional hit man may use .22 caliber ammo because they often are deformed, and the rifling is more difficult to determine. It also is easier to shoot accurately. This was a .22 Magnum, a bit more unusual.

The M.E. removed the brain and, using his Cattleman knife, made quick work of slicing and dicing for the pending tissue examinations. This appeared to be the same knife he used on the birthday cake when his pathology tech turned forty, and he threw him a party in the lab attended by four living and ten dead.

After collecting his clothing, and the bullet and taking some spectacular latent fingerprints, I headed back to the office. I enjoyed fingerprinting, as an old Greek veteran copper from the old and now defunct East Ann Arbor Police Department taught me the correct way. They were *spectacular* because the prints of living souls require a lot of manipulation of sweaty, resistant digits, palms, and egos. These were much easier; just roll on the ink and roll the print on the card.

Dr. Red then turned to me and said, “Curious to know if you catch someone, I’ll send you a report by next week.”

“Thank you,” I replied.

Making my way out to my car, I was grateful for others wanting to do all the cutting and probing, as it was not my cup of tea.

Saluting Officer Lenny, as I rolled out of the dock area, I called in, and dispatch said 10-5, which was code for “return to base and see command.”

Chapter 5

A few minutes later, I was at my boss' office, Captain RJ Lee. He was linebacker-size, with a thick neck and shoulders from weight lifting and nicely tanned skin from cruising out to his island off Lake St. Clair. He was late-fifties but had little gray hair or age lines.

His office was impressive. One wall was known as "the love me wall." It was lined with awards and commendations. All the dozens of framed at-a-boys were attached with fishing lines. One couldn't ask for a better boss. He explained the wall was needed to remind him when the "crap hit the fan," when the weight of the political machine was on his neck, and he and his unit was being unjustly criticized, at least he could still find a sense of accomplishment on the wall. Also, when he'd had enough, he could just cut all the fishing line, and he'd be ready to go.

I had a theory that how one treats their spouse and family reflected on how one treats his troops. He instructed me heavily in the area of relationships, as I was somewhat thick in the skull. Having a trio of boys, he knew they'd have to keep the bathrooms tidy themselves, washing the floors and the toilets regularly to clean up any messes. He saw it as a visible sign of love and respect toward the lady of the house.

He'd been hired right out of his fresh retirement from

the State Police, where he found his niche in creating a fugitive team designed to apprehend the "worst of the worst" criminals. To be effective in that job, he was a networker. He knew folks in the auto industry, banking business, credit card companies, phone business, and gas and electric companies. He knew all types of folks, from the federal law enforcement agencies to state and local cops, contacts he could call on at a moment's notice to get intelligence on anyone coming into focus.

He encouraged us never to focus on our past achievements and would often say, "What are you going to do for us today?"

The Captain seldom, if ever, had anything but the "happy to see you" look on his face. He motioned me in and said, "It's our long-lost Sergeant Murphy tap dancing his way in here with an imminent arrest," as he sat munching on a handful of Germack brand pistachios.

I couldn't stifle my laughter.

I leaned against his credenza and walked him through the location and position of the deceased, the gun-shot between the eyes and stippling, the congealed blood, the delay in reporting by Buzzard, the unlocked and not alarmed tunnel door and boot print. Finally, there was the autopsy and the lack of any significant items of note except the recovered .22 Magnum, 40-grain projectile and the tattoos.

"So, this is likely a hit, like a professional job?" he said.

"Beats me, Captain. I think this will probably require a good eighty hours of overtime this pay period to scratch the surface of this."

"Sure," he said, "Your transfer has been approved, I'm thinking you may need to get fitted for your parking enforcement uniform, eh?"

He was grinning ear-to-ear once again.

"Okay then, I better get back on this case, alright?" I nodded, stepping toward the door.

"Oh, by the way," Captain said, "don't make a career out of this case. There are fifty more that needs work, too."

"Right," I said and made a hasty exit to my office, where the stacks of files and papers seemed to have grown overnight.

The phone rang.

"Hello, Office of the Marginally Gifted. Can I help you?" I said.

"Sergeant Murphy? This is Rita, the building services supervisor. I thought you might like to buy me breakfast at Angelo's."

"Hold on, Rita," I pulled out a $20 from the panel behind my handcuff case. "Sure thing, I'll meet you there in fifteen minutes."

On the drive over, I mulled over the need to replace that $20 and remembered the $100 in my badge case. I'd learned to be prepared from the Captain. If a case took you away without advance notice, you didn't want to find yourself short of funds for gas, food, lodging or the occasional procurement of needed information to solve the case.

I recalled one such time when a stabbing suspect was identified, and we ended up on the south side in "The Patch." A zone of stripped cars on blocks, too many boarded-up windows and walls tagged in red and blue by gangbangers looking to claim their turf and gain a reputation.

Our "target", in that case, had no wheels, so it was likely he may have gone home to his Momma to hide out. I called for some assistance from an undercover State crew. A half-hour later, a knock at the door brought us face-to-face with a lady who didn't hide her suspicions of who we were and why we were there.

"Whatcha want Mr.?" she asked in her most disgruntled voice dripping with a sarcastic tone.

"We just wanted to know if Perry could come out and play?" I said.

"Say what?" she replied. "What's he done now?"

"Obviously, we wouldn't be here if he hadn't done something wrong. Mind if we come in?"

"Yes, I mind, but I know you will whether I agree or not."

"Oh no, Ma'am, we always seek voluntary compliance first," I said as we started looking around at well-worn furniture and piles of clothing stacked against the one wall beside a partially filled laundry bag.

"So, where is he?" said one of the crew.

"I don't know, and I wouldn't tell you anyhow," she said before going tightlipped and glaring at us.

"You know, I recalled your name was Delilah from the rental contract, and Delilah is a pretty name, like Samson and Delilah." Delilah was a very musical name, so I repeated it under my breath before saying, "Delilah, I got this $100 bill with your name on it. Would you like to have this?"

She snatched it out of my hands and said, "Room 3, Adagio Suites."

"Thank you very much, you truly are a good parent." Thinking to myself: *How much would I take to sell out my own child?*

Twenty minutes later, we keyed the door, and our man was in mid-stroke with another Michigan Avenue Momma when all five guns were trained on him.

“Man, you got a warrant?” Perry bellowed.

“Man, you got life insurance, Sir, now keep your hands way up high, so your family doesn’t have to cash it in.”

Talk about *Coitus Interruptus*. The lady screamed, grabbed her clothes and ran out naked. Perry unwillingly submitted to the arrest, requiring an armbar takedown, and within ten minutes, he admitted, under Miranda, he and the victim were “looking to hit a lick in the Union.”

“I found an easy mark when someone left their laptop unattended, so we took it and traded up at Sam’s on State Street for a c-note,” said Perry. “We then got to drinking on the roof of the carport across from the administration building, and arguing with him, he calling me a ‘ho,’ and CJ punched me in the mouth, so I shanked his ass.”

I love it when a plan comes together. Case closed one adult arrest.

Chapter 6

So, it was back to work, as the gravity of homicide with unknown perps was far greater than the attempted homicide of one of our known underserved—I just might need more cash if Rita had some good information.

Rolling into the only uphill carport in the area, I called dispatch and let them know my location. As the sunlight caused me to squint, I noticed a bizarre bronze statue of a large figure, a medium figure shaped like a beer bottle and a small one. It just looked liked three globs of bronze. Another work of fine art compliments the Art School. I found Rita inside Angelo's at booth #6.

Rita was a forty-ish Japanese widow whose husband died on a construction site.

She looked depressed but was very chatty whenever I talked to her, telling me about her childhood growing up in Toronto before moving to the States. She supervised a dozen or so custodians in three buildings adjacent to the Hill. She was not well-liked because, as she said, "If you can't clean the floors so you can eat off them, you should be mowing lawns or shoveling snow."

Most of her staff was not that conscientious, so she was at grievance hearings regularly and was regularly threatened by her staff, but she had the highest ratings on the campus from the management. Rita also wasn't going to take crap from anyone. She was the daughter of an Army Officer who fought on the losing side in World War II and could take orders and give them without hesitation.

Speaking of ordering, she ordered toast and coffee, and I did likewise, only raisin toast. Normally I would have about 2,500 calories in one sitting here, but I was trying to keep the mental edge by staying slightly hungry.

She always called me Mr. Murphy, and today was no different.

"Well, Mr. Murphy, two nights before the concert at Hill, I went out to the Building Services van about 12:15 a.m. and saw a Jeep Cherokee backed into the U of M gold permit space. I did notice it had a Crestwood license plate frame... and a crinkled bumper on the left side."

"Did you get the number off the plate?"

"No, Mr. Murphy, it was gray and had a sticker in the rear window, just three letters, MAT or MAP, or MAR...I don't know."

"No kidding, but you are sure about the frame from Crestwood Dodge?"

"I'm sure," she said

"Was it occupied?"

"That night... this dark figure..." she said slowly. "I

couldn't tell if a man or woman or anything else."

"You said, 'That night,' why?"

"Well, Mr. Murphy, I saw the same car the next night, but this time no one was in it, and it was by the loading dock at Mason Hall."

"How do you know it was the same one?"

"Same sticker, same damage and color, but no one was inside." Rita held her cup up in front of her mouth.

"Did you happen to look inside?"

"No, I had a load of supplies to drop off," she said.

"Ever seen this car prior to the night before?" I said in between bites of the sumptuous raisin toast.

"No."

"Think you could identify it again? Maybe it was just someone picking up one of your staff after work?"

"No, I look at who's coming and going here, and I've never seen that car before or since."

"Well, if you do, page me immediately." I scooped up the check and started to rise. "Oh, just one last thing. Any reason for your staff to be in the steam tunnels?"

"No, they're alarmed, and the last time, about a month

ago, one of the new guys was wandering around and opened the door. The uniformed guys came and talked to him, and I gave him two days off for being out of his area and not being where he was supposed to be."

"The guy you suspended, could he have been in the Jeep?"

"No, he transferred over to the hospital about a week later."

"Anyone else with a Jeep been in the tunnels, or do you have missing keys?"

"They don't have the tunnel key, so it had to have been unlocked when he opened the door and set off the alarm. All keys are accounted for, and I don't think anybody has a Jeep, but I'll let you know."

"I'll need his name and other information on him."

"I'll have it for you in about an hour."

"Thank you as always, you're a big help."

I shook her hand and offered her a smile. Rita, if anyone, was a model citizen. I wasn't going to patronize her by handing her money.

There would be other times for that.

Chapter 7

En-route back to the office, my cellphone went to autodial, and I called one of the area's more notorious ink slingers: Mickey the Tatman. I'd met him through my son, who came around with a new tattoo every time he passed through town.

Mickey was a tall, thin dude with a very sickly pale pockmarked complexion and quarter-size abalone disks in his ear lobes. He chain-smoked unfiltered Camel cigarettes. An avid fisherman, he told lots of fish tales whenever he'd come by to see "my golden child." His father had passed but had been in Law Enforcement in Ohio. Another thing he had in common with my son.

As an Ink-slinger, there was none better.

When the phone went to voicemail, I left a message about how he should give me a call very soon.

Chapter 8

Upon returning to the office, I informed Captain Lee of the progress made and hiked up to dispatch to check the parking ticket file for the car Rita saw. I also chatted with my favorite dispatcher supervisor, Darcy. She'd actually joined the department a few months prior to me and prided herself on knowledge of communications, emergency management operations and training all the dispatchers to a higher level than they'd previously attained. She was cool under fire and was reassuring with everyone outside of her arena—a true professional.

She was a middle child and grew up in a very traditional family that looked out for one another, and her faith was crucial. I knew she could handle herself and had more respect for her than most in patrol-land. I was grateful we had dedicated dispatchers, as they would send the troops into very volatile situations without ever knowing the outcome; they never had closure on much.

Darcy, like all the dispatchers, was overworked and underpaid and blamed first for lots of things she had no control over, such as crappy radio equipment and delays on LEIN or info from other departments, as well as not having been trained as a police officer. I actually wrote a 160 page thesis for my Human Resources Degree on the perils of burnout in their position and advocated for higher wages. I included a comparison study of other abysmal Big

Ten police dispatch wages before they bound their souls over to the union devils for security but no increases in pay. I gave a copy to the Chief, who never read it, which proved my case exactly: the culture very much discriminated against those in support roles.

"Darcy, how goes it?" putting on my best smile as ordered by the Chief.

"Sgt. Murphy, what's up with the stupid Cheshire Cat grin?" she said and curled her lips and nose and fingers similar to her own cat. "You want something, or are you just here to annoy me?"

"Darcy, you know you're my favorite and, yes, I'm here to annoy you," grinning, even more, causing my face to ache.

"Murph, you working on the dead guy in Hill Auditorium?" she said.

"No, I saw a very hot coed and thought you'd run the plate for me, so I could hook up with her and ruin thirty years of agonizing bliss."

"Violation of LEIN laws, Murph," she countered.

"I know that, I'm just testing you."

"You're testy alright," grabbing the card.

She first ran it locally on the parking ticket file, searching by the time of day for the week prior and any lots in the vicinity of Hill Auditorium. "Here's one 23:11 hours, 3-15-17, Parking Officer Hee ticketed a grey, four-door Jeep, Michigan tag ZXA. 954. In Lot C-1. Dumb luck, buddy, SOS is down," Darcy said.

"Well, let me know. Is Hee working today?"

"So, you think we know everything in dispatch? Not my day to watch him,"

"Okay fine," still grinning as instructed.

An hour later, I tracked down Officer Hee. He was out on the service drive between Hatcher and UGLI hanging paper on a half dozen cars parked in the fire lane. After legally parking my car in the service vehicle space, I approached him as an irate student was just starting in on him: "Fucking Nazi, I bet you get a big thrill out of ticketing my car?"

"No, not a Nazi. Samurai ticket-man. No, maybe shagging your girlfriend... but no thrill writing tickets."

"Asshole," said the guy.

"If you feel you were treated unjustly, go to the parking bureau and complain." Officer Hee smiled.

"Fuck off," the guy shouted.

"Another satisfied customer, eh, Officer Hee?" I

interjected.

Hee smiled and laughed and said, “College students, Shit for brains. I don’t know how these students get into college. Instead of ACT, GRE, or SAT exams, they should have to take a parking sign test.”

“With letters and words, or just symbols?” I laughed. “Either way, they’d flunk it.”

“What can I do for you?” said Officer Hee.

“I’m working on the guy who died in Hill Auditorium back on 3-17. I see you wrote a parking ticket on a grey Jeep in Lot C-1 on the 15th. Do you recall anything about that, things in the car, any distinguishing characteristics, anyone else around it?”

I handed him the department copy, and he looked at it.

“Sarge, I write forty… fifty tickets a day, especially in these lots around the Diag.”

“What time do you normally call it a night? Isn’t your shift 1600-2400 hours?”

Bending his current ticket book in half, he said, “Yup, they’re on my day-sheet: Time, lot number, ticket sequence.”

“Do you recall anything about that particular day?”

“Yeah, Sarge, it was the Ides of March.”

“Very good, so you like history?” I said.

“Sorry, I do recall that night when I was across the Diag at the Hatcher dock, one of those maintenance guys said he tried to back into a spot in C-1 and almost struck a car parked over the line in one of the spots. That’s why I went there.”

“Do you know the guy you talked to?”

“No, I don’t know his name, but I know he works out of Hatcher.”

“Thanks, you’ve been a big help,” I said.

Chapter 9

Back at base, I checked in with the Captain and asked him if he'd like to join me in working the case.

"No, but I understand you've been smiling more?"

"Oh yes, since the boss man told me I had to," I said. "You know I really love doing that."

"Well, perhaps you could do it a little less enthusiastically. People are starting to talk about your mental state."

The overhead speaker then went off: "Sergeant Murphy, call dispatch."

I grinned at the Captain and ambled back to my office, sitting on my desk as I dialed dispatch.

"Murph here. Could I speak to Darcy?"

She answered the phone.

"Darcy, what's up?"

"Your plate came back stolen out of Wayne, MI, sometime between 3-14-17 and 3-15-17. I'll put it in the outgoing DB box."

"Thanks. I don't care what your troops say about you, I still appreciate you."

"Bye, Sarge."

I found another souvenir mug from one of the many conferences and workshops I attended, this one being the 6th Annual Michigan-Ontario Identification Conference, where I learned all the specifics on the Toronto slayings of two young teen girls by a demented couple who kidnapped, raped and tortured them to death just for fun. It made me so glad I had a son instead of daughters. Good conference, but it had aged the Canadian cops.

I grabbed the mug and headed to the Bunomatic for my sixth cup of coffee for the day. Then I was out the door. First stop: Mickey the Inkslinger.

Chapter 10

Mickey's tattoo parlor was set in a strip mall on Packard Road in East Ann Arbor. This neighborhood was mostly homes when I first moved to the area. Back then, there were trees up and down this intersection but no more, just concrete and buildings now.

The anchor store in the area had been a less-than-appetizing private food market that sold discolored meat and fruits that were food for flies. Their vegetables looked like wrinkled old folks. The building had the appearance of a house that was added on to it. My brother worked there for a few months as he drifted from one coast to the other, trying to find himself. He'd been in town when a waitress from our favorite late nightspot was murdered.

I had to wonder, as it wasn't uncommon for drifters to run afoul of the law and prey on women working late. Eventually, the suspect was identified as a drifter serial killer who had killed a number of women in Michigan. The market was long gone, replaced by a chain retail store.

I arrived to find Mickey concentrating fiercely on inking an aqua and red feather along a young lady's scapula.

"Greetings, Mickey, got a minute to help me with a tattoo?" I said.

"Sure, won't your son be surprised? What do you want?

How about a tattoo of your son on your chest?" He smiled, all mirth.

"No, thank you. Just take a look at these photos and see if you recognize anyone's work."

Mickey sat up, still holding his tattoo needle. He peered closely at the photo and said, "You take these pictures, kind of fuzzy, isn't it? It sure isn't your son's work. The bird with the talons looks like Sid's work over at Ink For Ever."

Mickey stood, grabbed a pack of no-filter Camels and offered me one. I put my hand up and shook my head. Mickey lit one up and took a deep drag. He looked at the second photo. He turned it horizontally and then vertically. "This one, this is a military tat. My old man had one, got it Vietnam. It's a special ops tat. You won't see this on many people." He took a drag on the Camel and said, "The hood had a little fold in it, and that was the signature of Leon Durocher."

Mickey walked over to his computer and pulled up a photo of his father with a half-dozen other soldiers wearing sleeveless BDUs. It was plain to see that same tat on his right upper arm.

I thanked him and headed out.

Chapter 11

I was happy to get to drive to Wayne PD and then to Crestwood Dodge, and then to the lab. Traveling the back roads to the 2nd District State Police Lab this sunny spring day with the dogwoods, trillium and the jack in the pulpits blossoming, I realized how fortunate I was to be in this position thanks to two guys who saw much potential in me.

I went into the lab and dropped off the evidence, and ran into the director of the lab who was coming in as I was leaving. He went by the name Red and didn't appear to be over thirty but was closer to fifty, with an athletic body, neatly trimmed mustache and steely blue eyes, but no red hair.

His nickname came from working with blood, as he was a serologist by trade and could tell you fascinating things about forensics. He had a PhD, thought of himself as a scientist, and had published several articles—even co-authored a book on blood splatter. Red taught around the area at local colleges and, rumor had it, had the admiration of the female coeds.

"Ah, Sergeant Murphy from the U?" he smiled inquisitively.

"Yes, Director." I returned the grin I'd been practicing, and it felt uncomfortably fake.

"You know, most of us, including myself, are partial to the State University. Everyone treating you alright here?"

"No complaints," I said, waving to him as I headed out the door.

It took me a long time to learn the head guys don't ever want you to bring them a problem without bringing them acceptable solutions along with it; otherwise, you end up being the problem. Actually, the best leaders were risk takers and mentors who focused on coaching and encouraging others and could articulate the vision and goals of the organization. They stood along with their troops to get them where they needed to go. My Captain frequently reminded me, I can buy you a fish dinner, or I can teach you how to fish, meaning he could teach me how to be dependent on him or teach me how to be a trusted mentor to others and learn as much as I could to be more effective in my job and have a satisfying career.

Chapter 12

Forty-five minutes later, I was at Wayne Police Department in the office of my old academy mate William Alfonso Laberdie. "Billy Boy" was not the sharpest knife in the drawer back then, but he had a plethora of jokes and was a former college football player, so he had mobility, agility, and hostility, which worked well in the streets.

A year into his tour of duty, he disarmed a deranged twenty-year-old holding a four-month-old baby in one hand and a machete in the other hand. This was the makings of a suicide-by-cop, but Billy Boy had his partner distract the perpetrator and caught him from behind, ripped the wee one out of his hand like a football on the gridiron and put a wristlock on the perp, disarming him. All said, he walked away with a medal of valor.

"Sergeant Murphy, what can I do you for?" Lieutenant Laberdie inquired.

"I'm working a shooting, and there was a car of interest that was reported stolen out of this jurisdiction. I could use a copy of the report."

"Absolutely," said the Lieutenant.

Billy Boy. "What happened to the rest of the people from your department that were in our Academy?"

I replied, "They worked for a while and got in trouble

and got the boot. How about in your shop?"

"One stayed and got a medical retirement three years ago. The other person went to Warren PD, " said the Lieutenant.

Billy Boy went through the report and related that he didn't know of anything that could help us. The owner reported a bicycle stolen two years ago but had no other contact with the police. It looked like a straight-up steal, as no one at that address showed up in their database. I thanked him, we chatted about people we knew from back in the day, and then I left.

Chapter 13

I found myself on South Wayne Road looking at a well-kept bungalow just south of Annapolis. The door was open, and the screen door was latched while inside, the TV blared. I knocked, and a bald white guy about fifty appeared at the door.

"What do you want?"

"I'm Sergeant Murphy with the police at the University. I'm here about the car you reported stolen. Are you the owner, and what's your name?"

"Darryl Muscato."

"We had a crime, and your plate was seen in the area."

"Oh, *that*. What are you doing out here?"

"Can you describe your car?" I asked.

"It was a 1999 gray Jeep Grand Cherokee. I was going to sell it, but the only offer I had was from this punk that lives kitty-corner," pointing toward a white two-story house with a lot of junk in the drive way and no car present.

"Were you or anyone out at the U of M in the last few days?"

"No, I wasn't, but I have a nephew who lives here."

“What’s his name and birthdate?” I said.

“His name is Joseph Antonelli. He was born right after 9-11. My old lady and I divorced when she got bored of being married to a guy who sells tires and shocks. He’s my sister’s kid and pretty much keeps to himself since she got killed in a car crash three years ago. He’s a good kid, works over in Canton at the Tim Horton’s.”

“You had any issues with him? Does he use your car?”

“No on both counts. He has a Harley Fat Boy.”

“How about the punk across the street? What’s his name?” I said.

“Roger Stoddard. He got indignant when I wouldn’t take $500 for the Jeep.”

“What do you mean?”

“He took it for a test drive for about four hours and burned up all my gas, and when he brought it back, it had a crease on the side of it. Then it turned up missing a day later. You know, you ask a lot of questions. The cops here didn’t ask anything.”

“I’m sure they would have had the case been big enough. Are the police over there at all?” I nodded at Stoddard’s house.

“Sure, if it isn’t the noise, then he’s racing up and down

the street or fighting with his mother. He's just a punk, he needs his clock cleaned. Listen, Sarge, I got to get out to the shop."

"Thank you, Sir. Could I ask two more things of you? What day and what time did he take your car?"

"It was the 15th, 'cause I reported it stolen on the 17th."

"About what time?"

"I got home about 9:30 p.m., it must have been around 10."

"What kind of car does Stoddard have?"

"He drives a cherry red Camaro."

"Thanks, you've been a big help."

No need to go to Crestwood now. I thought.

Chapter 14

Lunchtime. One of my favorite things about running all over hell's half-acre was finding local food. I called my adopted son Matt who sorts mail for a private carrier, and he joined me at Brownies on Michigan Avenue. There wasn't a waitress under fifty in there, and they all wore starched uniforms that hung below the knee and spoke the King's English and gave service with a smile, unlike the disinterested, unwashed, tattooed rabble of the Republic's youth that walked around in a state of perpetual entitlement.

My favorite was a gal named Vi for Violet. She served you good food, lots of it, and was very attentive, telling jokes, asking questions, and always glad to see you. She seated me in one of her booths. I always tipped her well, as I suspected most customers did.

Matt showed up and was also treated regally by Vi. Matt and I went back a few years; he was the son of a government worker in the middle east. He grew up in Bagdad, where bombs exploded regularly.

He said, "Twice, I felt the blasts, and the noise was deafening. People died right in front of me. I needed to get away from that. I had some family come over too, but the Iraqis that settled in Dearborn were not kind to us, so we moved to the Republic."

I sat in rapt attention, knowing this was something that would change one forever.

We ate and talked, and he shared his interest in law enforcement as a potential career. Now is probably a better time to start than when I dove into it back when there were five hundred applicants for every one job. Now, every agency has recruitment fairs to get enough cops to fill their ranks.

Matt said, “Back to work for me.”

I’ll talk with you at the weekend,” I said.

Taking a few minutes at the 94 service drive for Metro airport, watching the planes comes in and making a call to dispatch, I talked with Darcy again.

“Hey you, how’s it going?” I asked.

“I was fine until you called. Have you no one else to bother?”

“Yes, I’m on a big caper and need you to run this first name R-O-G-E-R, last name S-T-O-D-D-A-R-D, age twenty-six, every which way out of Wayne?”

“Sure, anything for you; just put it in writing.”

“I broke my hand, and I’m out in Wayne trying to find the pieces, now, will you just run the friggen name and not give me so much guff.”

"But Sarge, I only give what I get," Darcy replied. "Roger Stoddard currently has a bench warrant out on him for failure to pay fines and costs for driving on a suspended license. He also had a felony conviction for receiving and concealing stolen property and possession with intent to deliver analogues."

"Great, thank you. You can have my autographed baseball signed by the '68 Tigers should I not return today," I replied.

"Just remember you owe me big time for this, gotta go."

The line went silent.

Chapter 15

Fifteen minutes later, after calling Billy Boy from Wayne PD and requesting a patrol car, I set up down the street from the Stoddard house and thumbed through the latest issue of MACP magazine I'd grabbed off the pile of department mail.

A half-hour later, a patrol car slowly made its way up Annapolis with lights and sirens going in pursuit of a cherry red Camaro. I drove up to the stop and waved my badge.

"Sgt. Murphy here, is that Stoddard?' looking at a red-haired pocked-marked kid who looked sixteen instead of twenty-six.

Officer Peters—according to his nametag—replied, "That's him. We got warrants. Lieutenant said you wanted to talk to him. Give us a half-hour, and you can interview him." The other officer had him out of the car, handcuffed, and was going through his pockets. He could only be described as scrawny.

Back at their station, the interview room held soft hues on the walls with Seneca false-face masks in each corner concealing cameras. Instead of the typical steel table and two chairs, there was a stool with a back on it, the legs were on rollers and a stationary chair for the interviewee.

Stoddard entered as the arresting officer uncuffed him

and then closed the door to the interview room. He flopped into the stationary chair. He shifted nervously, and his complexion grew more ruddy as he diverted his watery eyes from me.

I'm with police at the University, and the day you test rode your neighbor's car, you got a ticket out on campus."

"So you came here to collect on a parking ticket, how much is it?" he said.

"Twenty-five to life," I said. "Perhaps you can do something to help yourself ease out of a life sentence?"

"For what, grand theft auto?" Stoddard whined as his voice rose an octave, getting increasingly irritable.

"Auto theft is the least of your problems. You watch Forensic Files, Roger?"

"No," he said.

"Real cases, solved by scientific evidence. The juries won't convict without lots of forensic evidence, and you, my friend, just had a few tons of it dumped on you. Let me have you fill out this Miranda form unless you got something to hide?" I said.

"No, I didn't do it."

"Do what?" I queried as silence filled the air.

I kept reading, and when I got to the last line, *"having*

these rights in mind, do you wish to talk to me now?"

"Whoa, for a parking ticket?"

"No, Mr. Stoddard, will you answer some questions?"

"I'm none too bright, but I guess I'll talk to you. So, I parked illegally?" he said.

"And hit a truck?"

"He parked too close," Stoddard replied.

"You want to sign the form, like nice and voluntarily?"

"Is this about hitting the truck?" Stoddard said.

"That and other stuff, like murder."

"Okay, give me the pen. I didn't murder nobody."

"Any reason you'd kill someone while you were out there?" I asked, cutting to the chase as a good 5% of all crimes are solved if you just ask the right question right out of the gate.

"Sure, I shot him between the eyes," he said sarcastically and leered at me.

"So, jokingly, you shot him between the eyes as it appears that's how he died."

"No, I do property crimes, I don't hurt people," he fired back.

"Do you know who murdered this guy? Who was with you?"

Stoddard tried to turn the chair away, but it didn't move.

"There's a lot of physical evidence, so explain to me who was with you and why you were out there?"

"A couple of years ago, Joey and I came out here. He made a couple of keys. He worked temporarily as a custodian, so he had access to everything, and he stole this gold coin. He had me hold the keys he copied."

"Go on," I said.

"So, I came out to look around."

"Really, you ever heard of Pinocchio? Did you know your nose grows every time you lie?" I stared him in the eye.

"Why? I didn't do anything."

"You need to explain yourself because your DNA ended up not far from the parking space. I also will be matching some other evidence at the crime scene."

"Look, dammit, I didn't do it,"

"Do what?"

"I didn't kill nobody." Stoddard now looked scared, with an odor of fear emanating from him that told me I was on the right path.

“Roger, who was with you?” I asked quietly.

“Look, I know this girl, and we just went out there to hang out,” again, turning away.

“She has a name? What’s her name?” I asked.

“Beth”

“Beth, what?”

I don’t know, I just borrowed the wheels so I could meet up with her, try for a little nookie.”

“Really? Well, stud, so how did that work out?”

“I tried, but she told me she’s a dyke? It figures she’s a bug in the joint.”

“Where were you at?” I inquired.

“I was in Oaks up in Manistee. She worked at Scott Correctional, up in Northville.”

“Where’d you meet her?”

“My mother knew her sister and thought we should get to know each other.”

“What’s the sister's name?”

“Carleen Smith,” he said.

"Smith? Are you sure you didn't just make that up? Don't have me chasing down rabbit holes, sonny," I said, kicking back my chair as I stood and hovered my overly large frame over him.

"What you going to do, hit me?"

"Hell no, you watch too much TV."

The room fell silent. It was that pregnant pause that I really enjoyed, during which I gave him a look of disbelief and told him I'd be back before locking him in the interview room.

Billy Boy was down the hall by their booking counter.

"Well, Murph, did he confess?" "He will," I said.

"You all are way too nice. We could tune him up for you," he said with his affable grin and slight nod of his head.

"No thanks."

The look on Billy Boy's face was the same smirk two troopers wore years earlier when I'd called in for assistance to arrest a guy up in Brighton, maybe ten years earlier in my third department—when I'd dabbled with patrol work. I'd just sat down to eat the fried rice special at The Rendevous, a 24-hour greasy spoon on the edge of town. Dispatch crackled over the not-so-handy talkie: *SL 598, go to 821 Walker St, see the woman about a CSC.* An eight-year-old who was being babysat had claimed her stepfather molested her constantly. "I rolled on the call, and this child was so matter-of-fact right down to all the gory details of being molested, but reported it with so little emotion - I could hardly believe the child's flat affect. There was an emptiness in her eyes as she spoke.It told me something about shock and trauma.

I knew others who'd suffered childhood sexual abuse, and the shame and sense of helplessness were so unbearable they'd had to shut off their feelings—how else to survive multiple assaults? And maybe I'd shut off certain feelings too. How else can you see an eight-year-old in that kind of pain without breaking apart?

Stepdad had raped her for three years whenever she wanted to go to church, telling her she was a *dirty little slut and a tease* and needed to have something to confess, so he would force her to perform "oral sex" on him before dropping her at church.

He worked afternoons ten miles from my bailiwick in a window factory, and the local State Police post lent me troopers who covered the doors and assisted on the arrest. It was a hot sunny afternoon, stifling in the plant, and I felt the sweat spreading beneath my T-shirt, bulletproof vest and uniform shirt.

I'd thought for sure he'd bolt and run, so I walked in with his foreman, who made the introduction. We chatted, and when I got near him, out of earshot of others, I told him,

"You're under arrest," and put a wristlock on him and walked him out. I whispered in his ear, 'See my uniform? That distinguished expert medal for marksmanship on my chest means you'd need to outrun a .357 hollow point moving at 1250 feet per second. So... you willing to try? Your choice?"

He clenched his teeth, and his eyes flashed wide, and he just nodded.

Not too many pedophiles are willing to fight it out with you.

Once we got to the cruiser, one of the troopers said, "Hey Murphy, you should grab some coffee, and we can tune him up for you." The grin on the Trooper's face let me know he wasn't joking. The other Trooper tacitly nodded to approve of their plan. I thanked them both for their concern and the backup to the arrest, but I'd handle it from here.

I'd worked with multiple agencies over the years, and we all agreed our instinct was to rid society of this type of evil; but for me, I did it by the numbers, within the bounds of the law and policy. Staying true to my geographical imperatives to never go the same way twice, we took a number of back roads and ended up at the neighboring police department, where the jail bus picked up prisoners once a day.

It's hard to understand what it's like when you're sitting

that close to a man who's raped children, the two of you alone in a car, the thoughts that go through your head. How much closer can you get to pure evil?

I spent six-and-a-half hours with that pedophile, booking him, making sure he understood all the paperwork. He confessed on tape. A search warrant revealed exactly what she said would be there: dildos he'd used on her and her brother, Vaseline to lubricate their orifices, porno tapes he made them watch, and the Polaroid camera he used to take pictures of them for his trophy book.

The girl and her brother went to Children's Village for a while, and afterward I talked to their Mom, who said of her own daughter, "She always was a little tease... besides, I needed someone to help pay the bills." She said coldly.

The prosecutor wouldn't give me warrants on the mother even though she knew full well what was going on, but they stuck it to the stepdad. Mom died several years later from a ketamine-heroin cocktail.

The prosecutor thanked me at the preliminary hearing and said the defense attorney told him they had no wiggle room, which was very satisfying. Between the physical evidence, the statements of her and brother and his confession, a no contest plea got him

17-35 years in prison, of which he did 22 years. I lost touch with the young girl but always wondered how much the trauma affected her life and impacted her relationships.

I always wished I could have done more.

Chapter 16

Billy Boy's attitude about "the tune-up" only resolved me to do this case by the numbers, with no funny business.

At 1300 hours, I returned to the interrogation room, where Stoddard was slouched in the chair. My three-ring binder hit the floor with a thud, which jolted Stoddard upright. He ran his hand through his unevenly clipped red hair, and his complexion now turned red. He had on a paint-splattered t-shirt and blue jeans and a rawhide lace around his neck.

I sat about two feet away, staring intently at his face. Head turned to the right, so he didn't have to face me, he glimpsed at me with his peripheral vision. It was a full seven minutes of silence before he turned his head and said loudly, "I didn't do it."

"Do what?" in my most fatherly voice.

"I didn't hurt anyone," he said, quieter this time.

I moved my chair back and said, "I can see the grief this caused you. It's going to be okay. Just tell me how it happened?"

"It was Beth, We had a few drinks at the Crestwood Lounge. We drove out to the campus. I let her in the Natural Science Building, and...she went into the tunnel and came back a few minutes later."

"How did she know he'd be there?"

"I don't know."

"Bullshit. You knew, with that slender figure of yours and all those horny dudes in the joint, those prison wolves looking for fresh chicken meat, you won't stand a chance. You'll be somebody's bitch as soon as you get out of quarantine."

He played stoic for a minute, his face a stone. Then I saw the slight crack, the way his brow furrowed as he considered his future more deeply.

"What's her last name?"

"Hawkins, Beth Hawkins."

"Where does she stay?"

"Around."

"Accessory to Murder is a life-in-prison offense. Do you want to go away for life? Tell me you'd love to because that can happen."

"Listen, she had the gun." His voice rose almost to a wail.

"This story isn't making sense. You randomly go to the campus with this woman you know who has a gun and let her into the building, and she knows where to find the victim in the building? Doesn't make sense, Stoddard. How did you all know he was there?" I said, feigning that I was losing patience—we had all the time I needed.

“She called him, and they planned to meet in the basement men’s room.”

“Why?”

“I think it involved money and guns.”

“You think… money and guns? Yeah, go on.”

“Well, she knew people who wanted them and would pay a lot for them, so she’d get them from him.”

“Sure, that makes sense, Stoddard. But why kill him if they have this cozy relationship?”

“I don’t know,” shaking his head.

“So, what happened to the guns?”

“They were in a gang-box on wheels.”

“How many?”

“Twenty-four MP-4’s in Cosmoline.”

“Stoddard, you know a lot more than you’re telling me. Who else was with you?”

“No one.”

“What about the guy? Who was he?” I said.

"She called him Zack, I don't know any more than that."

"What's the motive here? You two just shoot him and rip him off?"

"She was mad at him. Zack screwed her sister. She got two things out of it, revenge and fifty-grand in guns on the open market."

I leaned forward and asked, "What did you get?"

"Nothing, I mean, she gave me a C-note."

"Where are the guns?"

"Don't know," he said.

"Where was she trained?"

"I don't know."

"That's bullshit because you know *some* details, so cut the crap, or I might lose my patience. You're up to your eyeballs in this, but someone may throw you a lifeline. Where are those guns? Or maybe I'll reconsider the offer and let the local cops deal with your lack of cooperation? Or maybe you can come out of this as a model citizen? What do you say?"

"Beth said there was this business in Inkster. Down on Inkster Road, below Michigan Avenue. A clothing store used to be a funeral parlor, and she was able to stash them in the basement."

"What's the name of the store?"

"Irv's Clothing and Tailoring."

"Did you help her put them in there?"

"I've said too much."

"Come on, if she's *that* connected, you may catch a bullet in your melon, too. What's Zach's last name, and what do you know about him?"

"Don't know. He likes the symphony. It was a good cover to do business."

"Or murder. Where's the gun she used?"

"Couldn't say."

"Bullshit! Think about it. Do you know what happens to snitches? They get stitches. Or worse! Can I get you coffee... a pop?"

"Coke."

"I'll be back."

I left the room and called my buddy in Human Resources at the Department of Corrections.

"Jan, how's it going? Murphy here at your Alma Mater. You retiring soon?"

"Five years, what can I do for you?"

"I need all you can get me on a Beth Hawkins who worked last at Scott Corrections. Just call me on my cell when you can get it. It's kind of a big caper."

"Okay, I'll fax it all over to you as well. Just send me the official request sometime today."

"Thanks, how're the boys?"

"Jason's a senior at State. David will be graduating from Holt in the spring."

"How's your son?" DOC Man asked.

"Working in Manhattan at a College."

I hung up and called the Symphony and spoke with Lynette. "Hey Lynette, did you hear about death at Hill last weekend?

"No."

"I need you to run anyone named Zach in your database, and he likely buys season tickets."

"There's a patron named Zach Arnold. He's the only one."

"Do you know him? Can you describe him physically? Got an address, phone, birthdate?"

"Large guy with a beard, early-fifties. Is he the one that died?"

"Can't say."

"He lives on Concord off Geddes. Born April 4, 1965. Married to Sasha Henderson, one of the violinists."

"Thanks," I replied.

Chapter 17

I called the Captain to brief him.

"Hey, Boss. We got an ID on the victim, some leads and a motive for a suspect. Film at 11."

As I pulled my car out onto the Avenue, my phone rang.

"Sergeant Murphy, may I help you?"

"Sergeant Murphy, this is Sasha Henderson. I was wondering if you could help me find my husband?"

"Sure, but why not contact the local police?"

There was a pause, a pregnant pause. I thought the line went dead.

"Hello, hello," I said

Almost a whisper in a very flat voice, the caller said, "My husband is Zach Arnold."

"Where can I meet you?" I asked.

"2644 Pittsfield, in the Village."

"Okay, see you in thirty minutes."

Built in the late forties for college students, the Village was a clean moderate place to start a marriage, and when my Bride and I moved there, it was our first abode together.

Despite having to park on the street, we had a quiet two-bedroom townhouse for $160 a month. Later, after we moved out, the Village "went condo," and the prices soared to over $120 grand.

The sky darkened as I pulled up in front of the condo. It looked like rain, and therefore unlikely I'd get to take a long walk with my wife tonight.

In the years since we'd lived there, they'd painted over the white-shingled siding, making it gray and brown, but had done little else with the condos. I walked up and knocked softly on the door, and a well-dressed woman in her early fifties answered.

"I'm Tim Murphy with the Police," I said.

She waved her hand, motioning that I should come in.

"Sit down, please," she said, moving her violin case off a very well-worn Thatcher leather settee. Looking around the living room and then seated, I noticed on one wall some summer scene photos of her when she was younger, along with a man and two girls on a dock at a lake. The room smelled of cinnamon and cloves, which I traced to scented bundles in a Lingenfelder basket on a sideboard in the dining area, which contained a mahogany table and straight-back chairs.

Scanning the room from my vantage point, I saw stacks of music manuscripts piled on an ebony-finished Steinway baby grand piano behind the sitting area. Figurines of the various composers adorned the room. A vintage 1950s Philco cabinet television stood on another wall. There was an absence of soft, easy-type chairs in the room. Three steps up were two bedrooms and a bathroom. One bedroom door was closed, but the other bedroom contained a double bed with a lilac-colored duvet fastidiously covering the bed.

I'd done enough death notifications to last a lifetime, and, at times, I recalled Verdi's comment to be compassionate, and one could *fake it til you make it*. I had to think to myself: what happens when you tell someone their loved one was murdered, and you need a lot of information, but all they want to give you is emotion?

"You and your husband live here?" I asked.

"No, his house is up on Concord off Geddes. We hadn't been getting along, and I moved out. Do you know where he is? with a puzzled look on her face?"

I thought for a moment and decided to just be straight up with her. "Ms. Henderson, your husband was the victim of a homicide."

Unlike the death notification of the widow Daly, there was no outward anger here, just a sadness that hung heavy in the room. I knew I needed not to say anymore. I only needed to be present, and I was fine with that.

After a long pause, Ms. Henderson spoke, “Can you tell me what happened?”

I wanted to tell her what we suspected, but that would come in due time.

“Why weren’t you getting along?” I queried.

“It’s a long story. He wasn’t faithful, and I found out about it. It wasn’t his first time.”

“Can you tell me about last Saturday night?”

“He called me and said he had something he wanted to tell me. So, I met him before the performance for dinner at Escoffier across the street. We had a quiet dinner, and he said the “whore” he slept with wanted money, and he didn’t want to pay her anything… his business wasn’t doing well.”

“What business was he in?”

“He was a district rep for the Great Lakes Casket Company. He loved classical music—part of why I was so attracted to him. He knew so much about music and came to all my performances.”

“Do you know who the other woman was?”

“No, I didn’t know her. One of my colleagues told me she ushered during our performances from time to time. She saw them hugging each other once. To think this was going on right under my nose was really upsetting, and now this...." She covered her hands with her face and sobbed.

There was never a good time to ask, but I knew it would save a lot of time investigating. I put it out there: "I must ask you, did you kill him?"

If she denied it and it came out later she had, it wouldn't hurt the case.

"Me? Heavens no. I didn't like him for his behavior, but I still loved him and was hoping we could work things out."

Her response didn't by any means eliminate her from suspicion, but I needed to know a whole lot more.

"Did Zach have any scars, marks, or tattoos on his body?"

Ms. Henderson nodded *yes* and asked, "Where is he? This is a nightmare!"

"Ma'am, I realize it is. He's in the morgue. I can take you there later, but it would be a lot of help if you could describe him for me."

"He had a tattoo on his right forearm; it was a hooded guy. He said he got it in Vietnam when he was in the Marines. He said each guy in his unit had the same tattoo. He also had what he called a screaming eagle' on the cheek of his buttocks."

This jarred my recollection. I suddenly recalled a biker

with the Devil's Disciples. I'd met him in the St. Clair County Jail, and he had the same tattoo of the hooded figure. He was about the same age and said he was in the First Marines during the Vietnam War and that everyone in his platoon had the same tattoo. The biker told me his unit was known as The Marauders and their orders were always clandestine missions deep into enemy territory that involved lots of killing and blowing things up.

She hadn't stopped sobbing. Reaching for a hankie, she wailed loudly.

I kept the questions coming.

"He ever speak of anyone wanting to harm him?"

She caught her breath, dried her eyes with the hankie and said, "Zach, he was always gentle around me, and I can't imagine him hurting others, but he *was* a warrior, a soldier who said very little."

I catalogued her response as the term *warrior* rang strangely, a little out of context.

My pager vibrated; it was the Boss.

I excused myself and stepped out onto the porch just as it was starting to pour.

The phone rang eight times before he picked up.

"Captain Lee, how can I help you?"

"Murphy here, I'm doing a death notification, interviewing the dead guy's wife."

"Get back here with the info as soon as you can. You know, the media, the PIO, is poking at the Chief. Where are you now?" said the Captain.

"I'm on the east side?"

"East side of Detroit? Flint? Bay City?"

"No, the east side of the Republic," I said. "I'd like to finish what I'm doing. Can we brief at 4 pm? I got to check some stuff before I come in."

"Make it 3:30. I'll get them all together."

I returned to Ms. Henderson and gave her a card, and told her if she thought of anything else about his habits or behavior to call me, and I'd be back in touch.

"OK," she said.

Chapter 18

I eased myself into the Toyota and realized the big hand was on the 15 and the little hand on the 3, and I needed some protein. I made my way to Depot Town at the Old Town Restaurant on Cross St. and took a window seat in my favorite booth. This neighborhood goes back 150 years. Red brick buildings alongside the rail line and in a valley along the river were the transportation arteries that were the lifeblood of the community. One abandoned brick building was a barracks for the northern troops during the Civil War.

The area held secrets of decades gone by—a murder of a young boy never solved, numerous shootings and stabbings when the festering biker gangs appeared to take over the local bars. Other colorful ones were: Ike the Barber, Jimmy the Dancer and the middle-aged local historian that walked everywhere and always kept his shirt collar buttoned even in 90-degree heat. He wrote a few books and was an authority in the area. There was a freight house that housed a coffee shop and farmer's market, and on Saturdays, local string bands filled the air with sweet melodies.

I entered the Café, and within seconds Loretta greeted me, "Detective, chicken noodle soup?"

"For the Soul or the Belly?"

"The belly—I didn't think you had a soul."

Loretta was in her early fifties with thinning blonde hair and the most beautiful manicured hands of a teen. She had the whitest, straightest teeth and a beautiful smile and green, alluring cat eyes. With wit as sharp as her nails, she married a "Chock Full of Nuts" restaurant supplier who wooed her away from a score of years at Brownies on the Avenue. She knew how to tell stories of interest about all that went on now in the two blocks in Depot Town and in the five blocks along that stretch of Michigan Avenue in Wayne.

"Tell me, how did you come to work here?" I said.

She sat down in the booth and said, "I started at Brownies around October '68. My jerk-of-a-husband had run off with a stripper from Bogarts. We lived just down the street. I was left with two little ones and needed a job. I went there when Fred Millton bought it, and I was there till he was selling out, and the salesman conned me into coming here."

I slid a picture of the rebellious Roger Stoddard across the booth. One glance and she said, "He's such a problem child, used to come around with Joey...what's his name? I just can't recall right now."

"You see him with any girls?"

"No, just racing that red car of his around the lot and up

and down the avenue." She stood smoothing her apron. "I'll get your soup." Minutes later, she was back with my order and said, "Joey's aunt had that coin shop down the street, and she knew Roger really well as he was always trying to sell stolen stuff to her."

"Ok, thanks, Loretta, I have to run, stay safe."

Chapter 19

I made it to the office in twenty-five minutes, walked a hundred yards to my office as I waved to everyone through a window and practiced my shit-eating grin.

My Captain motioned me in, and I sat down on the corner of his credenza.

"What do you have?" he said.

"This is odd; I just came from Wayne and talked with this guy who was out here the night the deceased, Zach Arnold, was killed. He knew this gal named Beth Hawkins, who was with the State Department of Corrections and said he drove her out here and likely she killed this dude who was attending the symphony at Hill. Afterward, they moved some MP4s to their car and off to a clothing store in Inkster. She had connections to get rid of the guns but was pissed at Arnold for banging her sister."

"How did you come by all this?"

"My investigative prowess," I replied, smiling—a real big one.

"You know the boss will want you to give this to MSP or the Feds?"

"I suppose he will, but that's where you and the DC need to lean on him. I thought you all loved me and wanted me to be happy?"

Rolling his eyeballs and scratching his bald head. He said, "Be down at his office in five minutes, got it?"

"Ok."

I walked out and sauntered down to my office, grabbed a bunch of messages from the desk, picked up one of the ten souvenir coffee cups and walked a hundred yards to the front office, ever so slowly, waving and smiling at everyone.

I walked into the Chief's office, and he looked up and said, "Sgt. Murphy, what the hell are you doing in Wayne? Do you ever work in your own jurisdiction? You want to work all over the state—well, go join MSP if you can get in."

He glared at me.

I glared right back. "Sorry, Chief. I kept my supervisor informed, and that's where the leads took me." I offered one of my smiles and said, "Besides, I'm not sure MSP is ready for my advanced skills."

"Captain told me all you've been up to. We thought you should have some help, sort of put together a team so we can explore all the parameters of this case for the best prosecution. Where are you headed next?"

"This had something to do with two-dozen MP4s, which are allegedly in Inkster. So, I thought I'd go knock on a few doors there and get them back. You want to come with me?" smiling as I sipped the tepid morning brew from my MOIA souvenir cup.

"No, I'm not going with you," increasingly more irritated, "and it's not good to be out there by yourself. You do this on your own, or are you planning to let Inkster know?" The Chief raised two fists and plunged down his thumbs as if to dismiss me and my ideas.

"Chief, of course, I'll let them know. I'm going to make it to retirement. Do you think you all could call Bernie over at FAT (the State Police Fugitive Apprehension Team) and see if they could put together a crew that could meet me at Irv's clothing on Middle-belt Rd. in Inkster? You do want this solved, don't you?"

"We will have you work with some folks, and you keep your Captain informed on everything. Do you understand?" he bellowed, the vein popping out on his temple.

"Sure thing, Chief." I gave him my very best cheesy grin.

Officer Marie was standing in the hall talking with Jimmy Rock, a veteran motor officer from Detroit, and Rock was saying, "We need a union-badly. No protection here."

Officer Marie turned to me and said, "How about it, Sarge, you with us?"

I choked on my lemon drop and one more swig of the

cold coffee. Shaking my head, I said, "Bad management breeds unions, but I've never found them useful. I can speak for myself, and if they want to mess with you, they will, and then you can sue them.

"Myself, I'm going to get disciplined at times, it goes with the job, but I see their side, and hopefully, they'll see mine. Remember, there are a half-dozen attorneys around here that are like vultures going after carrion, and the top brass knows it. They expect to open their purse and payout from time to time, it's just a matter of how much and how long it takes. In the meantime, do your job, keep on the sunny side, and you'll be retired before you know it, twenty-to-thirty years from now. If you're having a tough time, I'll listen to you."

I wandered off down the hall, looked in the alcove and saw an obvious bullet hole in the wall next to the copy machine. Corporal Louie de Ville Martels was exiting the training office, and I said, "Tell me, Frenchy, you all practicing your quick draw down this way instead of on the range?

"Say what, Dick-man? The Midnight Captain was bored, so he thought he'd have a shoot-out with some invisible gangsta and almost ruined our best copy machine."

"No, this seems crazy, a commanding officer discharged his weapon in the office?" I said with my usual sarcasm, "I can't believe it."

We laughed.

“Maybe he just needs more range time, “I said.” Good thing he didn’t hit the new live scan machine. Did he report it?”

Frenchy replied, “Have to give the man credit, he called the Chief first thing this morning and told him what happened.”

“Shazaam! Who’d have thought those copy machines were a threat? I’m feeling quite anxious now and may have to take stress-related leave,” I said. “Maybe safer on the street than in here.”

Walking into my office, I looked out the window and saw a squirrel eating a nut, barely a foot from the other side of the glass. My first instinct was to blast him, a fantasy that was interrupted by my ringing phone.

“Sergeant Murphy, may I help you?”

“You’ll like this,” said the Captain. “FBI agent Sean O’Malley heard about your plight and has offered to keep you out of trouble. What do you think about that?”

“So, the Feds think this a big enough case for them? Thanks, I’ll keep you posted.”

O’Malley was distinguished-looking, early-fifties, with silver hair and a mustache. He was always dressed to the nines; three-piece suit, a tie with a double Windsor knot, matching breast pocket handkerchief and watch chain and fob, and, of course, the FBI Academy ring. However, he claimed the best clothes were made of hemp. He was one of the last hired by J. Edgar himself. He and I worked a bank robbery together some eight years prior.

In that case, an *unsub*-unidentified subject robbed the teller of $4,300 at gunpoint at an on-campus bank branch. It was one of eleven banks robbed in two months in a three-county area. He drove a black subcompact SUV. Our break came after the last heist when a guy who owned a car painting business took his daily receipts to the bank, and a sharp teller noticed many of the bills were dye-stained. She called the Feds, and only one guy had paid in cash; an ex-con who with a registered black subcompact SUV, although by then, he'd painted it gold. He lived in an apartment less than a mile from the police station. A surveillance crew set up on him.

The Feds obtained a search warrant and invited me to join in on the fun—and fun it was. The hall door and frame were steel, part of the BOCA code to prevent fires from spreading from apartment to apartment and one-inch deadbolt locks (the Republic's ordinance), so the tools of choice were a battering ram and Halligan bar.

We'd arrived at the appointed hour with shotguns, fully-automatic rifles and pistols. The crew chief yelled, "FBI, search warrant," waited the prescribed time period of exactly one second, and then the ram went through the casing “like butter.” We rushed in, and the perpetrator was just coming out of his bedroom, all bug-eyed, looking as if he’d just soiled his $200 jeans.

Terror—that was his look. And he wore it just like his victims probably had It was a beautiful thing, so unbecoming of a six foot - six inch, 280 pound Nubian who looked to be a tough one to take down but wore shame and guilt on his face. However, that was always the danger of executing search warrants and making arrests, especially on a perpetrator’s turf—that always concerned me.

In those cases, the *unexpected* was the norm, and the adrenaline rush was better than sex.

I even had my own raid vest and did everything by the numbers according to my training. It was a “psych game” in which one was constantly anticipating the worst, yet that mindset kept me healthy and gave me a better chance of getting to retirement. You act cavalier in this business, naively assuming there’d be no resistance, dismissing the thought that your wife might just end up a widow. Still, decades of fast food lunches and late-night bar calls were tougher on my heart than a raid. Most of all, they were fun, especially because the bad guys were always more surprised and scared than we were.

Our guy had been alone in the apartment. We tossed the place. The bedroom was interesting as our man was making his own porno films. There were a set of lights and three cameras placed at different angles. The shelves were full of raunchy films.

A search of his closet yielded a rich bounty. This guy was an obsessive, compulsive neat freak. He had dozens of shirts, all of them with stylized razor cuts, the garments organized by color. His jeans had all been ironed and creased. I thought *The man had little to do if he had time to make all this happen*. A jewelry box revealed lots of gold rings and bracelets, ¼ and ½ karat diamond rings, ear studs and tie tacks, and two genuine Rolex watches.

Next was a chest of drawers. On the wallet in the caddy were business cards. The scene was a caricature of the perp's lair. This guy's name was Lance Williams, GA, LFT. I shouted, "Hey Mr. Williams, what're the letters for, you a licensed family therapist?" "No." He spoke in soft tones, his pitch quite high for a guy this size. "It stands for Gentleman and Aficionado, Lover of Fine Things."

O'Malley and I did all we could to keep from laughing.

We opened a drawer to find his shorts and t-shirts were all pressed and folded and on the edge of a line. Maybe our guy had a military background—or was it just a result of having been institutionalized? Was his OCD response to having no privacy in the joint? At least he could control his appearance and his clothes.

O'Malley and I looked at each other and thought the same thing: *You got something to lose, and we got something to use.* This was his OCD. Then we found a footlocker with a padlock on it.

Lance Williams sat up straight on the edge of his chair, handcuffs behind him. A big swarthy-looking agent dubbed Guido asked, "Where are the gun and the money? Our hunch is it's in the footlocker. You know, if you don't open it, we may have to go through everything and make a big mess. Who knows what might get damaged."

"Okay, okay. Don't mess with my stuff. Those shirts are Gucci and Versace."

"Really?" I said, thinking of my Value World two-for-$5 Wednesday specials.

"So, did you jack somebody for the Rolexes?"

"No, I bought 'em. Unlike you, I patronize fine establishments," said Williams, with a burst of indignation.

"I find great things at Value World, but unlike you, I use my own money. You know... my very own money I worked for and didn't have to steal?"

Williams just turned his head away, and suddenly an agent broke the lock on the footlocker and splintered the lid. Inside were neatly sealed bundles of cash totaling 11,807 dollars, some dye-stained, and a Crossman.177 caliber CO2 pistol.

Eventually, Williams pled guilty to one even though the

evidence was there tying him to *eleven* bank jobs, and he received six-and-a-half years in a federal penitentiary.

Typical resolution.

For O'Malley, though, everything was karma. He was flamboyant and talked incessantly, and I listened to the lame stories of his international love life. Overall, he was fun to work with and had resources I didn't have. I called his office, and Marie answered. She was the *real* Special Person in Charge. She knew more about them than she wanted to but kept the local field office humming along like a fine timepiece—maybe even a Rolex.

I asked for O'Malley and was transferred.

He picked up on the second ring.

"FBI, O'Malley."

"Murphy here, how's it going?"

O'Malley spoke slowly. "Pretty fair. Heard you got a big caper there on campus. We should talk. How about lunch at Bennigans tomorrow, 11:30 a.m.? There's a real hot waitress working there."

"No can do, Sean. Seems we need to move today as the word is there are two cases of MP4 rifles in the basement of a clothing store in Inkster."

"How do you know they're still there?"

"An accessory to the murder provided this information. It's less than twenty-four hours old. He's locked up at Wayne PD."

"Give me some horsepower on him, we may be able to use him as a CI (Confidential Informant) and leverage more information," said O'Malley.

I gave him all I had on Stoddard.

Chapter 20

Two hours later, we were sitting in a parking lot across from what appeared to be a funeral home with a large glass window full of mannequins dressed in the latest threads. I wondered if they actually put the bodies on display so those paying their last respects could do a drive-by a second time, just in case the first drive-by wasn't enough of an insult. The neighborhood was the Post-Nuevo-Dresden look of run-down homes and boarded up businesses, and trash everywhere.

We entered, and by the look on the faces of the staff, they seemed to know we weren't from the "hood."

"Hello, I'm Carleton Gibbs," said an enormous man in height and girth, extending his size-fifteen hand, which looked more like a catcher's mitt, toward me. Gibbs appeared to be about fifty, with a noticeable jagged scar at the right corner of his mouth to just below his right ear. It looked as if a straight razor was the weapon of choice. He had the frame of a sumo wrestler; with his girth, it would require three pairs of handcuffs linked together. His voice was that of a basso profundo as he spoke, "Gentlemen, looking for a new suit, or the 411?"

I released my hand from his grip and said, "Tim Murphy, with the police at the U over in the Republic, and this is Agent O'Malley with the FBI." We both flashed our credentials, and then O'Malley leaned over and showed me a text: *HRT is here*. That was a bit of a relief as I'd previously felt a tightness in my back and legs that made talking difficult.

O'Malley smiled and said, "Mr. Gibbs, we have a search warrant for your business. Who else is here? You want to have them come out?"

It suddenly appeared that Mr. Gibbs had a cortisol dump from deep in the recesses of his amygdala, and he was going into a fight or fight mode. Beads of sweat appeared on his forehead as his eyes darted from side to side; his jaw tightened, and his hands clenched like giant slabs of meat.

"I don't own this place. Perhaps I should call the owner before you search?" he growled. "My nephew Cameron is downstairs, and my cousin Doris does the alterations- she's in that room over behind you," pointing to the office of the showroom.

The HRT squad entered in their Kevlar helmets, flak vests and long guns. Even when they are your backup, one feels a quiver for an instant to see them enter. They moved at lightning speed, two remaining in the showroom with rifles trained on a very thin, short, salt-and-pepper-haired woman who'd come out from the back.

Four others rushed down the stairs, the point man with his shield at ready as they entered the stockroom, and one yelled, "FBI, hands in the air!"

The man identified as the nephew, Cameron, had bulging eyes and was shaking from head to toe. He dropped to the ground, a dark stain of what must have been urine spread around the crotch of his pants. In less than ten seconds, he was handcuffed, helped to his feet and escorted up the stairs.

The team continued to search and found a half-dozen caskets stacked in one corner next to the breaker box. A step ladder was arranged so that one could get to the top casket lid. One team member escorted Gibbs downstairs.

"What's with the caskets?" O'Malley queried.

"They're left over from when this was a funeral home. We had no use for them."

"Oh yeah," lifting open the lid on the top casket, inside which I spotted several Cosmoline-wrapped long guns. "Then I suppose these, too, were already here when you moved in?"

"Maybe you should talk to my attorney?" said Gibbs.

"What for? You're not under arrest at this point, Mr. Gibbs. In fact, we're so grateful for your cooperation and would just like to know who put them here and who owns them?" I stood balanced on the ladder, still holding the lid of the casket open.

"I didn't know they were here. You've got to ask

Cameron."

Back upstairs, Cameron Gibbs remained handcuffed behind his back and perched on a stool in the main office. He was in his late twenties, with a light complexion and sunken eyes, mottled teeth and acne scars. He was dressed in a short-sleeved linen off-white shirt and pants and high-top black tennis shoes.

His right forearm bore a tattoo in cursive script reading: *I'm not much, but I'm all I got*.

"Well, Mr. Gibbs, what's it going to be? Your cooperation could set you free," I told Gibbs, flanked by two team members. "You'd do a long stretch in prison for these guns, and there's no good time in the federal system, but the one we're really trying to get to is the person from whom you got them—unless you'd prefer to be an accessory to a murder?"

Gibbs' eyes filled with tears; he was visibly sweating now. White spittle formed in the corners of his mouth as he spoke with an edge to his voice, "I don't know Jack, I don't know nothing."

"Ok, let's go," O'Malley said.

The HRT Team stood him up and moved him toward the stairs to the showroom.

O'Malley spoke, "Listen Mr. Gibbs, there may be a way

for you to work this out as a paid informant where no one knows who gave us the information, and you make some money."

"Don't clown me," Gibbs said with concern. "You put it in writing that I won't do no time, and maybe I'll say something."

"Or we could just finish this here and maybe take you out in one of the caskets?" said the point man.

Gibbs looked around the room, his eyes traveling from one heavily-armed agent to another, and I smelled something familiar: *fear*.

A common smell in this business, especially when interviewing someone who's scared. Pheronomes are chemical signals triggered in the brain in conjunction with the amygdala and hypothalamus. It's a telltale sickly and a vaguely sweet odor that always let me know I was on the right trail, that stress is overwhelming this person: It's a cue to double down and dig in more intensely. In the animal world, they pick up on this and sometimes go on the attack, their prey having chemically telegraphed the message: *come kill me.* Man's ability to perceive this is clouded by urban environments where the smells of nature are masked by pollution, exhaust, perfume and deodorant, obscuring the innate function of our nose. I found a connection with this sense was essential to successful interrogations. I'm always trying to locate the odor and use it to determine what the bad guy or gal did—and when they're about to break and spill their guts.

The sensation took me back to a suicide where a coed ingested cyanide and, as CPR was performed while waiting on the ambulance, the odor of burnt almonds filled the air, truly the smell of death.

Gibbs shook his head and said, "Okay, okay, all I know is this bitch I met through my cousin called me and said she wanted to store some stuff here until the weekend and gave me five bills. I didn't look in the crates and didn't know what she had brought in. That's it, that's all I know."

"She got a name?" said O'Malley. "How about a phone number?"

"Bethany, Betty—something like that. She called me on my cell, so there's a number?" He held up his phone.

"Where did you meet her?" I asked.

"My cousin Alicia knew her."

"Where'd she stay?"

"Down on Cherry St. in the townhouses."

"Give us an address and phone number."

Gibbs held up his phone again. I copied the address and phone number.

“Who was with this gal with the crates?” I asked.

“Some squirrely white dude driving a Jeep. Never met him before and didn’t know his name.”

“Until we straighten this out, you’ll be locked up. Got it?” O’Malley said.

The HRT team took possession of the caskets logging in twenty-three MP4s, and I checked my voicemail, where my buddy Jan from DOC had left a message.

Jan said that Beth Hawkins was a seven-year veteran of the Corrections Department and was suspended without pay as she had shaken down family members of inmates, and it had reached the Deputy Warden. She was currently staying at 5902 Faust St., Detroit. An unmarked unit drove by, and the two-story, white-sided house looked like every other on the block. A utility check was made, and the owner of the house was Randy Seidler, a guy with a long criminal history. A few of the highlights included running a house of prostitution, possession of analogues, and carrying a concealed weapon.

O’Malley and I exited the funeral home/ clothing store, talking on our way to the car. We agreed that Hawkins had a different Modus Operandi. So what was the connection with this Corrections Officer living with a convicted felon? Why the unusual type of shooting, the victim’s hands-free and shot between the eyes with a .22 Magnum caliber? This was not the typical hands-tied-behind-one’s-back execution-style shooting with a bullet to the back of the head.

Gun running and murder at the U, suicides with guns, hot-blooded domestic violence with guns, drug trafficking and murder to cover up other crimes—was this part of institutional higher learning?

Back at the car, I called the Captain, who said, "It might be good if you came back out this way someday... you know, to work?" When he spoke, I always listened carefully for the message behind the message—that was his style.

"You want to come out and play?" I said. "We're having a blast! Boss, I'm learning a lot about what goes in a casket—like guns, for instance—and we've gleaned intelligence like the type of clothes one should wear to a funeral."

The Captain remained silent.

"We found the guns, and the nephew of the owner of this shop is making 'statements against his own interest,' as the legals might say. This Corrections gal is living at the house of a convicted felon, so O'Malley and his crew and I are headed over there."

"I'm sure he is," said the Captain. "And no, I don't want to come out there. I have to go to my kid's game. Listen, stay off the 6 o'clock news."

"Sure thing, Boss," I said, at the very instant my cell phone battery went dead.

Good thing I always carried two spares, as one never knew where one's travels could lead you.

Chapter 21

Daylight was starting to fade, and I thought I should check in with the family. One thing, among many, I learned from the Captain: “Family first.”

I remember me complaining to him about the cost involved after he extolled the virtues of taking the family to Disneyworld. I frankly had no interest, but the rest of my family was very excited, and so we went. Those pictures of the kids with Mickey, Donald and the gang and the thrill of riding Space Mountain with the boys were meaningful for both them and me as they grew up.

The line rang.

My bride, Pat, answered, “Where are you?”

“I’m in Detroit, just north of Fairlane. Thought I’d tag along with O’Malley and do a little early Christmas shopping at the mall,” I told her.

“You working late playing cops and robbers?” said Pat, as if this was a joke. “I’ll be home within two or three days,” I said. “No, I’ll be there to read to the Chortles (kids), check under his bed and in the closet, and kiss them goodnight.”

“Okay, stay safe,” she said. She knew what this job meant to me, the years of striving and how important it was when the big cases came along.

"Hey, the boys need milk in the morning, and we are out, please get some on your way home," she said

"Ma'am, Yes, Ma'am," I replied in my loudest voice.

Chapter 22

O'Malley pulled his car into the Ford Hospital lot. This became the staging area once the rest of his team pulled up. They went over how Larry would take the point, Moe would cover the back, and Larry and Curly would enter and right-to-left, room-by-room search inside. The last detail focused on notifying DPD of our presence in case they were needed.

The HRT point person knocked on the door and stepped to the side.

The door opened slowly, just two inches, revealing the head of a large-framed, dark-skinned man of about thirty who peered out with a surprised look on his face. One look, and he slammed the door. The crew reared back before lunging forward and crashing through the door.

We rushed inside.

A light-skinned female dressed in black ran up the stairs to the second floor. Everyone but two pursued her. Halfway up the stairs, I heard a deafening explosion, a sound like a bundle of M80s. It came from the back of the first floor. Then I heard a *pop, pop, pop* and an agent screaming, "FBI, face down on the floor!"

The commotion drew my attention to the front bedroom.

I ran to the doorway.

The woman, gun-in-hand, had slipped through the window and onto the roof as the HRT squad gave chase and went after her.

A squad member trained his sights on the woman and yelled, “Drop it or die.”

She tossed the gun, and it slid down the roof and landed in the gutter. She stepped back toward the window and then pushed off and ran to the edge of the roof and jumped a distance of fourteen feet to the ground. When she hit the lawn, she rolled twice, and when she came up, a squad member was on her taking her to the ground, twisting her arm with an expert warp-speed move. In three seconds, she was secured, face planted on the lawn. Another agent bound her with flex cuffs and her legs with a looped cord, and she lay there like a roped PBR rodeo calf.

Beth Hawkins was in custody.

O’Malley and I came down the stairs to the sounds of sirens wailing in the distance. We put her in the back of the car and pulled out as Detroit PD arrived to take charge of the scene. We waved at them and headed toward the Republic.

As a rookie detective, my mentor was a State Police detective named Lee Paulson. We first met when I was a contract security guard at the state unemployment office.

He and another man came in wearing trench coats and felt hats, asking about some out-of-state murderer who'd run off from down south and who was scamming the state out of unemployment money. I knew they were the police. Lee was a country boy from a hamlet up north. He was built like a linebacker, a country boy with a disarming smile and "folksy" approach—and he was just that folksy. Lee taught me a lot about just being a decent human being and not being an authority figure as a police officer.

I was always grateful as he stood behind me throughout my career. He and the Lieutenant helped me hone my skills as an Investigator, Interrogator and Supervisor. Lee sent me to the Reid School to learn what questions to ask and how to ask them. Reid had been a charter member of the OSS during World War II, the forerunner of the CIA, and he and a Chicago cop wrote one of the Bibles on interview and interrogation. His works were also based on a Chicago cop named Fred Inbou, who came up with a structured interview and interrogation techniques using Behavioral Analysis.

Some of their work was later discredited, but I was blessed to go through their training program, knowing full well that in court, one had to have a plethora of evidence, from forensics, expert and eyewitnesses, to all kinds of other information that a skilled prosecutor needed to sway a judge and jury and obtain a conviction.

All I learned would be utilized in a face-to-face meeting

with this young lady.

Chapter 23

O'Malley and I drove Hawkins back to the station, and she barely uttered a word, projecting a vitriol that seemed to express we were mortal enemies. We were ruining her life, and this trifling matter of getting arrested had not been in her game plan today.

So, here we were facing Beth Hawkins and wondering what would be the right question to ask, one that would pull a confession from her. That was my goal in life. I figured when I met God someday, I'd ask, "What is the perfect question? What would be the one thing I could ask that would bring out the soul of someone and allow them to talk to me without all the facades people put up?

I had dozens of questions to ask Beth Hawkins.

Interview room #3 was newly remodeled, and you could still smell the fresh paint on the walls. It had a video and sound system now and a camera in one corner, and a one-way mirror so the room could be monitored.

Hawkins was shackled to a steel loop on the table, and she sat looking in the mirror, making faces as if there was humor in all this. O'Malley sat opposite her, and I sat on the short end of the rectangle within two feet of her.

My training told me: *just ask her if she killed the deceased and why?*

"Ms. Hawkins, my name is Sgt. Tim Murphy, and this is Agent Sean O'Malley. We are investigating an incident at Hill Auditorium and would like your cooperation in this matter."

We knew so little about her, so I asked, "Where did you grow up?"

"I ain't from here... I'm from Evanston."

"What brought you here?"

Being slow and deliberate was, quite often, a successful formula for getting confessions. In other cases, I'd often just call the perpetrator at about 3 p.m. on a Friday afternoon and tell them their name came up in an investigation and ask if they'd come in and talk early Monday morning. That way, they'd worry about their role in the crime all weekend. By the time Monday rolled around, they'd be so nerve-racked it didn't take much to break them and unload all the details, implicate themselves in the crime and confess their part.

"Do you know why you're here?" I asked Beth quietly, in almost a whisper.

"Clue me in, Bozo?" She glared with a vengeance in her eyes.

O'Malley and I smiled at each other and then turned and smiled at her.

We sat in eerie silence.

She wouldn't be a pushover, but these long, strained pauses raised blood pressure and increased heart rates. Silence worked in gaining leverage.

After a seemingly interminable two minutes or so, I said, "You probably know the Miranda Waiver Warning, so we can get your side of the story. I'll read this to you, and you can sign it if you like."

She looked at it and signed it, and dated it with the time.

She agreed to talk.

"Your buddy ratted you out," I said. "He told us about Zach and the guns. Why did you do it?"

"Do what, Bozo?" biting the inner corner of her lower lip, nostrils flared and glaring at me with her red enflamed hazel eyes.

"Kill Zach?" I said, deadpan. "And, by the way, that's Sergeant Bozo to you." I looked her in her cat eyes and saw there were dilated pupils; her head was cocked to the side as if she was going to attack. "More importantly, your shot placement and choice of weapons intrigue us?"

"My buddy, eh?" she said. "Roger's a poser. He had to be put in segregation when he was at the Oaks 'cause he was snitching on others."

Posers were petty criminals who'd often tell huge lies in jail to bolster their credibility. I tended to like them but never believed a word they said. The rule on the street was: *Omerata*. In other words: the Code of Silence.

Beth didn't answer my question.

"Tell us about Zach. The man, do you wrong?"

"Not me, Bozo." She glared at O'Malley and then at me. "He messed with my sister and shouldn't have. She's only sixteen, and that guy was at least thirty years older, and we were tight, but then she said he forced himself on her. I thought *that's enough*, and stuff happens."

"What's with shooting him between the eyes and the weapon of choice?"

"This demon needed to be able to see his executioner," Hawkins whispered.

"So you became the executioner and shot him?"

"Didn't say that, Bozo," she said defiantly.

"Sgt. Bozo to you," I replied. "What's with the rifles?"

"He was in the casket business, and his warehouse by the airport was constantly under surveillance, so I said bring them to Nat Sci, put them on the elevator, and take them into the tunnel on a Saturday before the concert. I could make money and get rid of the bastard at the same time."

"I must admire your resourcefulness. Where's the gun you used?"

"I just changed out the barrels from .22 to 9mm."

"Where's the barrel?" O'Malley asked.

"I tossed it in the reservoir off Newburgh Road."

"We took the liberty of going through your phone after we got a search warrant,"

I told her. "We called your sister and asked her to come in so we could chat."

She pointed two fingers at me. "Bastards," she said. "Leave her out of this."

Chapter 24

When O'Malley and I stepped out of the room, he said, "Hey, Sergeant Bozo, what's your plan?"

"When this is done? I'll have to go buy some clown shoes."

Moments later, my pager vibrated the front desk number. I stepped out of my office and called the front desk.

"Sergeant, there is a lady on the phone for you. I'll transfer it."

The line switched over, and I said, "Sergeant Murphy, can I help you?"

"I heard you may know the whereabouts of my sister."

"And you are?" I asked.

"Charlene Smith, Beth Hawkins' sister," she stammered. I thought she might have a speech impediment. "I went by my sister's house, and the cops said you had her."

"Ms. Smith, can you come to the police station?" I asked.

"Yes, it will take about a half hour."

I returned to the interview room, made sure our star suspect was secure, posted a female officer with her, and

O'Malley and I went to the conference room to meet the bosses.

"So where are you with this?" said the Chief.

"One in custody, she made incriminating statements as to where the gun barrel is and a motive," I said. I learned years ago that with the Captain and DC, you could give a detailed explanation to showcase your stuff, and they were fine with it. But it was different with the Chief. He had this axiom, part of his orders; *Don't build me a clock to tell me what time it is*.

"Also, the guys got off a few rounds, but we were out of there before Detroit PD, and the news crews arrived.

"That's on the Bureau, and we will cover the press, " said O'Malley.

The Chief was not happy. His temple throbbed as he glared at me and clenched his fists. It was a time when a bushy mustache might have served him well.

I nodded to the Captain and DC and excused myself. Once in the hallway, I could see the knoll outside the window, and the sun was just beginning to set, reminding me that it was time to tie up some loose ends.

Chapter 25

My desk phone rang, and when I picked it up, my favorite dispatch supervisor was on the other end, saying, "This is Darcy, over at the front desk. You have a visitor. Charlene Smith. Shall I send her back?"

"No, I'll be right out."

I quickly strode the corridor, failing to wave and smile, and entered the lobby to meet a thin and short high school-aged teen wearing a blue Michigan sweatshirt and jeans. On her feet were pink running shoes. She looked up as I entered.

"Ms. Smith?" I asked.

She nodded and stood up.

` "Thank you, come this way," I said, ushering her into the interview room off the lobby. She sat down across from me in a metal chair.

"Do you know Beth Hawkins?"

"Of course, she's my sister. Her neighbor said there was some gunfire next door, and the police took her away in handcuffs," she said.

"Do you know the name, Zach Arnold?"

"He's my stepfather, married Mom ten years ago, but

they separated.”.

“Why do you all have different last names?”

“My real father died when I was six, and my mother married Zach Arnold.”

“What was your real father’s name?”

“Calvin Hawkins, but he was killed in a car wreck,” she replied.

“What is your mother’s name?”

“Sasha Henderson.” She looked off to the corner. “But that’s her maiden name. It was Sasha Arnold, but she filed for divorce.”

“Ms. Smith, do you know why the marriage was in trouble, why she was divorcing him?”

“My stepfather was awful. Two years ago, he started coming into my bedroom while I was sleeping and putting his hands all over me. I told my mother, but she didn’t believe me at first. It was getting worse—he molested me for over a year. I don’t even talk to my mother now, but I told Beth. She was crazy upset. She even said she’d take care of him.”

“When was the last time you saw Zach?”

“A month ago, down on State Street. I stay far away from him.”

"How is it that you have the last name, Smith?"

"I just use it to distance myself from others," she replied.

"Did Beth say how she would take care of him?"

"She didn't say. Why what happened?"

"Zach Arnold was shot." I pointed to the bridge of my nose.

She went blank, almost like that eight-year-old all those years before.

"Does your sister own a handgun?"

"Yeah, the gun the Corrections Department issued her, and she has another one."

"Do you know the caliber of her personal gun? Do the shells look like these?" I removed a magazine from my nylon carrier and showed her a .40 caliber S&W hollow point round at the top of the magazine. "Or something like this?" I asked, pulling up a photo image of a 40-grain .22 Magnum cartridge from an ammo book I used for reference.

"It was like that one," she said, pointing to the image in the book.

"Can you account for your whereabouts last Saturday between 4 p.m. and 2 a.m? Sunday morning?"

“I was with the Glaser’s until we went to the symphony about 7:30 pm because my mom had to rehearse. My girlfriend and I got to Hill, went to hear her play about 7:50, left the concert about 10:15 pm and took a cab back to my house.”

“Who’s your girlfriend?” I queried.

“Tiffany Glaser, we’ve been friends since middle school, when we played in the band at Tappan Jr. High. We do a lot together.”

“What happened then?” I asked

“We made some hot chocolate, called some other people we know, and then she stayed the night,” Smith replied.

“What time did your mother come in?” I queried.

“About 11 p.m.”

“I thought you didn’t get along with your mother?”

“I don’t, but I need a roof over my head at night.”

O’Malley coughed and joined in the questioning, saying, “Do you know who killed Zach Arnold?”

“No, I’m just glad he’s dead.”

“Understandable,” my brow twitched involuntarily. “Did your mother or sister kill Zach Arnold?”

"I don't know. I know they were very upset with him."

"Did you tell Tiffany Glaser or anyone else about Zach Arnold molesting you?"

Charlene stiffened, folded her hands and quietly answered, "No, it's not something you tell, or it would be all over social media."

"Do you know your sister's friend, Roger Stoddard?" I asked. "He was driving a Jeep or red Camaro."

"I don't know her friends. She told me she was staying on Faust Street in Detroit."

"How'd you get there?" I asked.

"Tiffany's Mom drove us," she said.

"Did your mother stay home with you two the rest of the night?" O'Malley asked.

"I don't know—I guess so." Smith shifted her position on the chair and ran her hand through her hair.

"Excuse us," I said. "We'll be back in a few minutes."

Chapter 26

Leaving the interview room, O'Malley and I walked the one hundred yards to the interview room occupied by Beth Hawkins and peeked into the interview room. Her head was down, cradled by her left arm, which was cuffed to the steel loop on the table. Her other arm extended across in peaceful repose.

We knocked on the Captain's door across the hall.

He waved us in.

"What's the latest?" he said, scratching his head, opening his collar and loosening his tie.

"It appears our victim was molesting his stepdaughter, and we've several suspects. Here they come One, the sister, Beth Hawkins; two, the mother Sasha Henderson; three, the victim Charlene Smith; four, Roger Stoddard who was with Hawkins in the gun running; and five, James Buzzard, the reporter and facility manager at Hill Auditorium."

"Okay, just stay off the news," said the Lieutenant. "I'm going home. Call me if you get a confession." He stood up, put on his jacket and left the office. O'Malley and I remained for a few minutes, going over all we had learned.

"We know all of them were in the vicinity the night he was killed," I said. "We can ask them for polygraphs and swabs for gunshot residue. That could help."

O'Malley kicked up his feet on the Captain's desk. "Listen, Sergeant Bozo. I like your new name, but don't you think these people wash their hands more than once a week?"

"You'd hope so, but it sure would make this go quicker if one of these folks had residue on their hands. On the flip side, if we swab and get nothing, the defense is sure to use that at trial."

"Okay, let's start with Beth Hawkins," I said. "She already said she threw the barrel away, so she had to disassemble the gun to change barrels and likely would have powder on her hands."

"Well, lets go for it," O'Malley said.

I went back to my office and called Billy Boy out in Wayne. He agreed to have Roger Stoddard examined, but nothing was found.

O'Malley and I entered the interview room and un-cuffed Beth Hawkins, took her down to lock up and used the chemical agent on her hands. Under the light, there were traces of residue, but that wasn't definitive proof she shot Arnold, even though there was a circumstantial case.

Next, we went and got Charlene Smith. When we examined her hands, we found nothing. We drove Smith out to her mother's house and followed her inside. She called Sasha Henderson, who wasn't home but was supposed to be back “in ten minutes.”

“Let’s wait,” I said to O’Malley.

Charlene disappeared into her room, and O’Malley and I sat at the dining room table. Framed on the wall were photos of Sasha with the Symphony. One photo had a group shot with the staff, but James Buzzard was in the photo standing next to Sasha Henderson—it struck me as weird that the facility manager would be in the photo with a bunch of musicians, particularly the same guy who reported the crime to the police.

I called out to Charlene, and as she walked into the dining room, I asked, “Who’s the tall, gaunt man in the photo?” Not that I didn’t already know.

“That’s Jim, the guy my mom’s been seeing,” said Charlene. “He was an old war buddy of my stepfather. He worked at Hill and started coming over after Zach left.”

The screen door opened.

Sasha stood at the threshold and peered in at us. She took care of her appearance, with shoulder-length auburn hair and a minimum of makeup and dressed in a beige blouse and matching colored slacks carrying a leather satchel and violin case.

“Hello, Ms. Henderson. Do you remember me? I’m Sgt. Murphy, and this is Agent Sean O’Malley with the FBI.”

They nodded at each other.

"We're trying to eliminate people we suspect. So will you submit to having your hands swabbed for gunshot residue?"

"Well, I guess," she said timidly. "Perhaps I should talk to an attorney first?"

"Ms. Henderson, tell me about the man in the picture?" I said. "Right there." I pointed to the photo on the dining room wall.

"He's a friend, the facility manager at Hill."

"What's his name?" O'Malley said. "What sort of relationship do you have with him?"

"His name is James Buzzard, and I met him through my husband. They were in the war together. He was always so quiet and shy, and we just go out for coffee and talk."

"Did he know about Charlene being molested?" I asked.

"Yes, Beth and James, and I talked about it. James was furious, even more than Beth. Ms. Henderson was very animated as her voice increased in volume to a crescendo saying, "How could he betray his own family?"

"Let's get those swabs so we can eliminate you, and then we'll leave you alone," I said.

"So you knew Zach was in the building?" I said.

"No, I only learned about it after the performance," said Ms. Henderson.

"From whom?" I asked.

"My stomach was in knots. I was sick all over about the fact he'd harmed Charlene. I hadn't stopped him. I felt I was a bad mother. I regretted my choice of men. Charlene was there with her friend, but so was Zach. I knew he'd be there in the audience, and James told me he was in the basement men's room." Ms. Henderson's voice was cold, almost emotionless. "I had Beth's pistol in my violin case and told Maestro I was ill just before the climax of the last movement.

I wanted him to feel pain and know how much he'd hurt us, so I opened the stall door, and there he was, sitting on the toilet. He looked at me, shocked and started to say something, but I was so focused, I pointed the gun at his face and shot him right between the eyes." She broke into sobs. "He just slumped over, and I could see on his face that he'd never hurt anyone again."

O'Malley and I looked at each other and just shook our heads.

O'Malley asked, "Where was James through all this?"

"He was in the hall outside the room, so no one would come in," she said.

"What happened to the gun?" I asked.

"I brought it home, and Beth got rid of the barrel."

"Where?" I asked.

"Don't know for sure, but she said something about a lake," Henderson replied.

"You know where?" I asked. "Did you know about anything else happening down the basement?"

"No, what will happen to Beth and Charlene?" asked Ms. Henderson.

"Don't know at this point."

I stepped outside and called dispatch while O'Malley stayed and kept an eye on her as I heard the sobs return a little louder.

Chapter 27

"Police, can I help you," said Darcy, my favorite dispatcher.

"This is Murphy, please put me through to the patrol supervisor."

"Oh you, are your fingers broken? You can't call him direct?" she said.

A moment later, Lieutenant Merritt answered with a soft, pleasant voice, saying, "Lieutenant Merritt here." Merritt enjoyed his retirement job at the University. He'd completed the minimum twenty-five-year career with the State Police.

"Lieutenant, we need you to send a Quad team over to Hill Auditorium for the facility manager. James Buzzard, Code 2. Have them take him into custody. Appears he was involved in the death at Hill. Very likely, he's armed. I'll call the prosecutor for a search warrant. We need to seize his phone and computer. Let me know when you get him in custody."

Lieutenant Merritt's tone was always one of calmness. "Right, Sergeant.," he said. "We'll move on it right away."

QUAD stood for Quick Action Deployment Teams and required four officers with heavier weapons than pistols, usually rifles and flak jackets and helmets. Buzzard was in for a shock.

Back to Henderson: we needed to transport her, and so she was searched and taken back to the station. Years back, in another jurisdiction I'd worked, an officer decided to transport a young lady in the front seat with no handcuffs. She pulled a small Raven brand .25 caliber semi-auto pistol from her bra and popped the cop in the temple. A mindless error on his part, which cost him his life. His picture hung on the wall in our squad room as a reminder to follow procedures. I never took chances.

Making arrangements for Charlene Smith to go stay with her Aunt and Uncle was another load off our minds. Imagine knowing your no-good stepfather had his brains splattered on the wall while your sister and mother are likely headed to prison for a good long stretch.

Oh, the phone calls and paperwork to be done.

Of course, the veterans always told me that "the case is made at the typewriter," or, in this case, the computer.

Chapter 28

We'd just finished securing Henderson in the interview room across from my office when my desk phone rang.

"Sergeant, Murphy here."

"Darcy here. Shots fired. Your presence is requested at the loading dock of Hill Auditorium."

I signaled to O'Malley, and seconds later, we were burning rubber on the streets of the Republic. O'Malley screeched to a halt on the sidewalk, jumped out by a wall just south of the building and as we exited, we heard the Carillon chime in the Bell Tower.

This brought back memories of a mild March morning years before: I'd been dispatched over to the Bell Tower on a "shots fired" call right when the Carillonneur was in the middle of a Bach Fugue. This was scary, as one of the first mass murders in this country took place at the University of Texas Austin bell tower when a deranged ex-Marine Sniper killed fourteen and wounded scores more and finally was shot dead by an Austin cop.

Upon arrival at the Bell Tower, one body was located on the ground. A witness said they'd heard a rifle crack, and then the body fell to the ground. It was a few hours of pandemonium. Due to the close proximity of the buildings and the reverberation, it was later learned that it was a suicide, a jumper their body had hit the ground with such impact it sounded like a rifle shot to the people in the area. I later used the incident to write a fifty-page paper on the physics of falling objects, analyzing terminal velocity.

When we arrived on the scene, a uniformed officer said to us, “Sarge, some witnesses said your guy fled into the Bell Tower with an M-4 rifle. The QUAD team was deployed. Since Buzzard was a veteran who knew weapons, no one was taking a chance.

Officers opened their car trunks and suited up with flak vests, Kevlar helmets, and M-4 rifles, as well as other officers uncased their Remington bolt action .308 sniper rifles with scopes in the event Buzzard, declined to surrender. Metro SWAT was also called, keeping pedestrians out of the area a major concern. Within another twenty minutes, the area was as secure as it was going to be, and negotiations began with the negotiator using a bullhorn and attempting to get Buzzard to talk. The theory is if the bad guys are talking, then they aren’t shooting. Also, should they express what they might lose, the negotiator then has something they can use.

Other responders took cover behind a wall by the loading dock side on the Thayer St. side of Hill Auditorium. O’Malley and I entered the building with the Quad team. A few rooms on each floor needed to be cleared of any threats. The elevator was shut down, so the stairs were the only option. We’d done this exercise a few times before but usually without anyone having live ammunition. Now it was the real deal, and we were after a guy who not only knew weapons but had killed before.

We cleared each floor and room all the way up to level seven very slowly. Time seemed to hang in the air. From the stairwell, the fire door to level eight was ajar and had us all on edge as we viewed the world through our green-tinted lazar sights.

O'Malley and I came up after the point guy and button hooked on the wall going into the Carillon chamber—where the console was played, which connected to the bells in the tower. The room was poorly lit, and the ambient light seemed barely enough to see the full expanse of the chamber. On any given day, this room produced the background music for the hustle and bustle of those moving across campus to classes.

Off to the south side of the room, we saw motion and screams as our target shielded himself with the Carillonneur. He had his left arm around her throat. He was a full foot-and-a-half taller than her. With his thin hair and sunken eyes, and gaunt hollowed cheekbones, he looked as ghoulish as ever. In his right hand, the muzzle of the MP4 was pointed at her neck.

My mind was whirling as I recalled all the steps in crisis negotiation. I heard my old instructors reminding me: *If they have something to lose, we have something to use*.

"James, drop the gun," said the negotiator. "There's no place to go, and it doesn't have to end this way."

As quickly as he swung his rifle barrel from the victim's neck toward us, two deafening flat cracks reverberated through the carillon chamber. The first one hit directly at the bridge of the nose. He actually seemed to freeze for a microsecond before the back of his head exploded, splattering his skull and brain tissue against the wall. The second shot hit him in the voice box, and there was a gurgling sound as he slumped to the floor behind the Carillonneur as she shrieked and cried out, "Oh my God, Oh my God."

She gasped and sobbed and fell forward to the floor but otherwise appeared unhurt.

The QUAD team rushed in and secured Buzzard. I stepped forward toward Buzzard's corpse and crouched to comfort the Carillonneur while O'Malley picked up his weapon and emptied it, and made it secure before handing it over to one of the team.

The remainder of the team tended to his body and ushered the Carillonneur out of the room while O'Malley and I stood looking out onto campus from the big glass window.

"You know Casey's over on Depot St., I know this gal," O'Malley said, "You want to grab some food before we start the paperwork?"

"Sure thing. You buy, and I'll pick up the tip," I said.

"Okay, Sergeant Bozo." O'Malley laughed and slapped me on the back.

I relayed to the team leader to post an officer and keep everyone out, call the Medical Examiner Investigator, and secure the weapon. I told him we'd return forthwith.

As we ambled down the stairs, I realized my pulse was down from over 180 to 130, which was not ideal, but grateful my ticker was another day closer to retirement.

We exited the building, and as we walked to our car, the Chief and Captain pulled up in his car.

"You two alright?" said the Captain.

I looked in and met the gaze of the Chief. He glared at me as his temple throbbed, and I smiled my best smile widely, almost making my face hurt and said, "I'm okay, how about you, Sean?"

"Okay," said O'Malley. "We're going to go eat something. You all want to come?"

"Will pass," the Captain said. "Just one question before you go: Who got shot, and there was either one of you involved?"

"Buzzard, the hostage-taker was fatally wounded and, no, neither one of us fired." "It was the Quad point, man,"

I said.

"Be back for a debriefing by 3 p.m., got it?"

"Yes, sirs," I replied.

Captain leaned out the window and said, "Good job, guys." And so ended another day of serving and connecting at the U in the Republic...

The Author

Tim Shannon is a retired police supervisor and currently a mental health counselor. He and his bride reside near Flat Rock, Michigan.

A2 Death Knell is Tim's first untrue crime story. Previously, he wrote *Hell, I Was There,* a story based on a score of letters written by a family ancestor who fought as a foot soldier for the North in the American Civil War.

A Detail Quiz

1. Are there 16 or 18 lights between the Murphy home and the crime Scene?
2. Is it Carleen or Charlene Smith?
3. What is the People's Republic?

Made in the USA
Monee, IL
10 July 2023

38914692R00088